MINE

TIES THAT BIND DUET

A. ZAVARELLI
NATASHA KNIGHT

Copyright © 2020 by A. Zavarelli and Natasha Knight

All rights reserved.

Cover Design by Coverluv

Photo by Wander Aguiar

No part of this book may be reproduced in any form or by any electronic or mechanical means, including information storage and retrieval systems, without written permission from the author, except for the use of brief quotations in a book review.

This is a work of fiction. Names, characters, businesses, places, events and incidents are either the product of the author's imagination or used in a fictitious manner. Any resemblance to actual persons, living or dead, or actual events is purely coincidental.

1

KAT

Sometimes, a smell will trigger a memory. Aftershave. His particular brand. Other times, it's music—like the heavy metal he'd play that sounds so much like the beat on the dance floor.

Tonight, everything has been made more intense by the vodka I consumed before we even got to the club. That and the little pill Nina gave me.

He's not here, I tell myself. *It's not possible.*

I'm being paranoid. And I need some air.

After making my way to the back of the club, I pull the heavy metal door open. I'm shocked by the cold air as the door closes with a clang behind me, shutting out the music and the people. Leaning against the brick wall, I look around and meet the eyes of a woman taking the last drag on her cigarette before dropping the butt and stamping it out under her boot.

She doesn't smile but neither do I as her boyfriend leads her back inside.

My head is spinning. Closing my eyes, I draw in what I hope will be a steadying breath. The cold helps, at least.

The door opens again, and I hear music and voices. Men's voices.

Opening my eyes, I straighten, my back stiffening when I look over to find there are three of them.

When they spot me, they stop talking to take me in, openly looking me over.

One grins, then steps forward. "Smoke?" He holds out a half-empty pack of cigarettes.

The nightclub is full, but we're the only ones outside.

"No, thanks," I say, pushing through them to catch the door and slip back inside before it closes all the way.

I catch my reflection in one of the mirrored walls and almost don't recognize myself with my new hair. Magenta. It was an extravagance, but you only turn nineteen once. I scan the club for Nina and spot her on the dance floor with a couple of guys.

She sees me and flashes a smile. I feel my mouth stretch into one too and touch my face. It feels numb. I've taken Ecstasy once before, but it didn't feel anything like this.

The music is getting to me. It's the constant beat. My heart is hammering to keep pace with it, and the smell of sweat and alcohol and too many people is making me nauseous.

I'm about to head to the dance floor to tell Nina that I don't feel good when the door opens, and the guys who were just outside come back in a waft of cigarette smoke.

When the man who offered me the cigarette sees me, one side of his mouth curves upward. He walks toward me, and his friends fall into step behind him.

"Hey, beautiful."

I turn to walk away, but one of his friends moves around to block me.

"Where are you going?" he asks.

I change direction, but the other one is in front of me now. I turn again, but I'm blocked by the third man. I feel dizzy as I glance beyond them to the dance floor, but I can't see Nina anymore.

He's talking again, the leader, but the music's too loud and his words sound hollow. I scan his face, then his friends' faces. They appear almost demonic, and behind them, the room is spinning in a sea of technicolor lights.

"Excuse me," I say, trying to push through the wall they've made to block me.

Their leader steps directly in front of me, cutting me off. When I back up, he plants his hands on the wall on either side of my head, effectively caging me in.

"Don't be like that. We just wanna have some fun."

"Look, I'm here with my boyfriend," I lie.

He leans toward me. "I don't see a boyfriend." He lets his gaze run over me. "In fact, you look like you're looking for one the way you're dressed."

I'm wearing black from head to toe, faux leather pants that hug my curves a little too tightly, a corset top, lace fingerless gloves that go halfway up my arms and high heeled, lace-up boots. Not out of the ordinary for this place although I did borrow the entire outfit from Nina and it's definitely not my usual style.

"Well, I'm not." I try to slip out from underneath his arm, but he just shifts his body, once again blocking me. "Get away from me."

"One dance with me and my friends. Right here. I'll go first."

Lights pulse around us, making me feel sick. I slump against the wall, unsteady in the high heels of the boots. I don't know what he reads in that, though, because next thing I know, he's pressed up against me.

"What the hell?" My eyes fly open, and I shove him. "What are you doing? I said let me go!"

"And I said one dance."

"Are you deaf?" I hear myself ask as I try to push him backward. The walls seem to be vibrating around me, the bass pounding against my head and in my chest. Or is that my heart? I need to get out of here. "I'm warning you to get off me."

He laughs outright, and his friends follow like monkeys. "You're warning me?"

"Yeah, asshole. I'm warning you." Without a moment's hesitation, I ram my knee into his groin.

He grunts, hunching over, and his arms fall away from me.

The instant they do, I whirl around and trip over his feet in my haste to get away. I'm sure I'd fall flat on my face if it wasn't for the chest of the man I slam right into.

"Whoa."

Big hands close around my arms, catching me before I go sprawling, and my nose smashes into the middle of his very hard chest.

I hear the jerk I just kneed mutter a curse behind me.

"Everything okay, sweetheart?" asks the man I just crashed into with an accent I can't quite place. It's familiar but not, and he smells good. Not like sweat or beer or cigarettes.

I blink, looking straight ahead at what would be his pristine white V-neck T-shirt but for the smear of magenta lipstick. It matches my hair and has ruined his shirt.

"I..." I take a tiny step backward because he still has me. I turn my gaze up.

And up.

The first thing I see are his eyes, beautiful and dark, and for a moment, I can't look away.

He pauses too, or I think he does at least. And when I smile, he smiles back, and a little dimple forms on his right cheek. It softens his features and brightens his eyes.

Then the room around him goes darker, the music and people too loud.

"I need to sit down." I sway on my feet.

He mutters a curse under his breath and catches me.

"My girlfriend's had a little too much to drink," the man from outside says as he grasps my arm so hard it hurts.

"I'm not—"

"Your girlfriend, huh? That's not what it looked like a minute ago," the one with the accent says.

I look at the hand wrapped around my arm and open my mouth to tell him he's hurting me, but before I get the chance to, the one with the accent shifts me, placing his body partially between ours. He doesn't even have to touch the guy to get him to let go. Even I can see he's bigger, badder, and his body language alone is enough to get the other guy to back up a step.

My knees buckle again, and he tightens his grip around me, pulling me into his side.

I need to find Nina and go home. I try to straighten, to pull away, but it's like my body won't listen to my brain. My feet tingle in my borrowed boots. My whole body tingles.

"What's happening to me?" I ask. I'm not sure anyone hears me because no one answers.

I squeeze my eyes shut, and I think Nina got the wrong pill. If this is Ecstasy, I should be feeling ecstatic, right? I just feel out of control.

"Get these idiots out of here," the one with the accent says, and I look up to see two other big guys move in behind the one I just kneed.

But then Nina's there. "Hey, you okay?" she asks, peering into my face. "Crap."

"I think I need to go home," I tell her.

She looks up at the one who has me, and a worried expression wrinkles her forehead. "Come on, let's get out of here," she says, but when I try to slip out of his hold, he doesn't let go.

"What did she take?" he asks Nina.

"Nothing. Just vodka," she lies.

I know he doesn't believe her from the silence that follows. "How old are you two anyway?"

My gaze shoots to Nina's. We're not twenty-one.

"We're just going to go," Nina tries to pry me from the man, but he won't let me go. His grip doesn't hurt, not like the other guy, but I know I'm not going anywhere until he allows it.

"Did you buy something off someone in the club?" he asks her as if she hasn't spoken at all.

Nina exhales, looks around, and finally nods.

"Who?"

"I don't want to get anyone in trouble."

"Who?"

She points.

"All right. Take her home," he says, and one of his men steps forward.

"I'm not leaving Kat," Nina says.

"Kat?" he asks.

At the mention of my name, I look up into his beautiful, dark eyes. The way he studies me, eyes so intense, I feel my face burning up.

"Kat's not going anywhere," he says. He's still looking at me, but he's talking to Nina.

I'm not? "But—"

"That man you bought from doesn't have permission to sell here. I don't know what you got, but I need to keep an eye on her in case things go wrong."

"Nothing's going to go wrong. I'll just take—"

"You know who I am, don't you, Nina?"

I wonder how he knows her name, but Nina just bites her lip and nods. I don't think she's surprised that he knows her.

"Who is he?" I ask her.

She just glances at me but doesn't answer.

"I don't want to have to call the cops," he warns.

"Cops?" I ask, suddenly panicked. We used fake IDs. We'll get in trouble.

"Shh. It's okay," he says to me, tucking me into his arm. His tone when he talks to me is different than when he's talking to Nina, and I get the feeling he's trying to keep me calm.

"Just let me take her home, okay? You can have one of your guys drive us if you want. She'll be fine. I'll take care of her," Nina pleads.

He doesn't answer right away. I think he's considering her request, and at that moment, I'm not sure what I want.

"I don't think so," he says finally. "Andrei will take you home. Kat will stay here with me."

"But—"

"Andrei," he cuts me off, looking over Nina's shoulder at a man I don't like the look of. "Take Nina home," he says.

Andrei eyes Nina, and I don't like the look on his face.

"*Just* take her home, you hear me?" he tells Andrei.

Andrei snorts. "Yes, sir." He mock salutes, then shakes his head. "Let's go," he tells Nina, grabbing her arm.

"We have to leave together," I try to tell him, but Nina's already walking away with Andrei.

"Relax, Kat," he tells me as Nina turns to look back at me over her shoulder. "Nina will be fine," he adds, and I look up to find him studying me again.

"I don't feel good," I manage, just as my knees give out. This time, he scoops me up in his arms like I weight nothing and begins to walk in the opposite direction of where Nina's going.

"You just close your eyes," he tells me. We're on an elevator a moment later. The doors slide closed, and at least it's quiet so I can think again.

"The music's too loud."

He looks down at me and smiles like he's humoring me. "You don't like loud music, but you're at Delirium?"

Delirium. It's the name of the club. Nina's been here before, but it's my first time. "Where are we going?"

"Somewhere you can rest."

I nod. I'd like to rest.

"Is Kat short for Catherine?"

"Katerina."

"Katerina." It sounds foreign when he says it. "Means pure." His face grows thoughtful. "You don't belong at this club, Katerina. You'll just get dirty here."

Before I can think about what he means, the elevator doors open, and he carries me into a large, quiet room. There are several doors leading to other rooms, and a large desk that's holding three screens that flash various images of the club downstairs.

He sets me on the couch. I watch the monitor that shows Nina walking in the parking lot, then getting into a car with that man.

"Nina?" I try to get to my feet on legs that feel like Jell-O. Nina and I have a pact. We come together, and we leave together. Always.

"Shh, Kat," he says. His hand on my shoulder gives me a gentle but firm squeeze. "Nina's fine. Andrei's going to give her a ride home."

"We're supposed to leave together," I tell him again.

"Not tonight."

He sits down beside me, and I'm glad I don't have to get up because I don't think I can stand.

I look at him, really look at him. He looks different up here without all those flashing, colorful lights. He has messy brown hair, and his eyes aren't as dark anymore as he studies me. They're warm now. Like chocolate.

I love chocolate.

Without thinking, I reach out and touch his face, feel the rough stubble of his jaw. He raises an eyebrow but lets me.

"Do you know what you took?" he asks.

I drop my hand when I see that pink stain of lipstick I put on his shirt. I try to rub it out, but he pulls my wrist away.

"It's fine. What did you take?"

I squint my eyes and shift my gaze up to the ceiling, trying to remember. "It looked like candy. It was my birthday gift."

"Happy Birthday, Katerina. How old are you?"

"Nineteen," I say without thinking, then remember my ID says I'm twenty-two.

I open my mouth to amend my answer, but the elevator dings, interrupting us. He stands up. I realize I don't know his name. I'm about to ask, but then the steel doors slide open and a man comes inside. He's carrying my coat in one hand and a little bag of those colorful pills in the other.

"That's them," I tell him.

They both look my way but ignore me, and when they speak, I don't understand a word they say because they're talking in a different language. Russian, I realize.

I lean my head against the back of the couch and close my eyes. I feel hot, and there's a residual thumping between my ears like leftover sound from downstairs. I wish it would stop, but at least I'm out of the noise and sitting down.

Someone touches me. Forces one eye open.

"Hey!" I turn my head.

"She's rolling," he says, then they switch back to what sounds like Russian.

When I open my eyes again, we're alone, and he's crouched by my feet undoing the laces of my boots.

"Awake again," he says.

I'm embarrassed to have drifted off.

He tugs a boot off, and it feels so good to have it gone. Nina's feet are half a size smaller than mine, and the boots were pinching my feet.

I watch his dark head as he unlaces the other boot and takes that off too, then stands. He might be the tallest man I've ever seen.

"You're beautiful," I tell him, laying my head on the back of the couch again.

"And you're tripping. Here." He walks away, then returns a moment later and hands me an open bottle of water.

I take it and drink a sip, then several gulps, realizing I'm parched.

He sits beside me, and I look down at what he's holding. It's my clutch. He opens it, and I'm slow to process as he takes out my things and lays them on the coffee table.

"Hey," I say. "You can't do that."

He ignores me, eyes my fake ID and pockets it, then studies the real one.

"Your hair's pretty. Why do you color it?"

I touch my hair, disappointed that he doesn't like it, and suddenly feel incredibly sad.

"Ah, shit. Don't cry."

I didn't realize I was.

"You're very beautiful," he says. "I'm just saying your natural red is very pretty already."

I smile, taste the salt of a tear, and lean my cheek against the couch again. I watch him as he takes a photo of something in my bag.

He thinks I'm beautiful. And I think he's beautiful.

I feel a grin stretch across my face, and I do something I would normally be too shy to do. I reach for his face with both hands, press my mouth to his, and I kiss him.

He's surprised, I can tell, but he kisses me back a moment later. His mouth tastes good, like whiskey but not stale, just nice. And the scruff on his jaw tickles my cheek, and I want him. I want him so badly, there's an ache between my legs and an emptiness inside me that I've never felt before.

But when I try to slide my tongue between his lips, he draws back.

"Hey, hey." He looks at me, and his eyes have gone dark. "You're high."

I'm confused, but then I look down, and I see he does want me too, so I smile at him. "I want this," I tell him and kiss him again.

This time, when he breaks our kiss, he groans. "Katerina," he says, his voice low and deep and like he doesn't want to stop. "Be good."

Be good.

Instantly, I'm transported in time, and that feeling is gone; that warm, achy wanting has vanished.

Be good.

"I'm sorry." I drop my head and pull my hands into my lap, then slide one up under my fingerless glove to press my nails into my forearm until it hurts. "I'm really sorry."

"Hey." He taps my face. "It's all right. You with me?"

I blink, rubbing my eyes.

"I don't know what you took, but you're tripping. Just try to relax."

He wipes his thumbs across my cheeks, and I see smears of black on his fingers. I turn my hands over and see how the backs are smeared with black. Smokey eye gone wrong. Nina had spent half an hour doing that. I wonder what I must look like now. A raccoon probably.

But then he takes my hands and draws them apart, and we both look down at once.

Shit. My glove.

I try to draw my arm away, to cover it, but he doesn't let me. Instead, he peels the glove off and turns my arm so he can see all of it. Every ugly, bumpy inch of it.

I look too, and sometimes when I see it, I can still feel how much it hurt.

But that's not important right now.

I put my hand over it, although it barely covers half the scar.

"I'm cold," I tell him.

He looks at me, and for a moment, I think he's going to ask me how it happened, but then, without a word, he's on his feet, and a moment later, I'm lying down on the couch and he's laying a thick wool throw over me. He lifts my head to slide a pillow beneath it. It's scratchy, but I don't mind.

There's a ding, and I think it's the elevator again. I try to sit up, but he tells me once again to relax, so I lie back down.

He pulls his phone out of his pocket. Must have been a text, not the elevator.

I watch him type something, then repocket it. He looks down at me. "Why don't you close your eyes for a little bit? I have to go take care of some business, but I'll be back, okay? You just stay here and get some sleep."

I nod. I am tired. Really tired.

He says something else, but I'm already drifting off, and I feel like I'm floating, like I'm lying on a soft cloud and just floating. I hear him talking again, but I can't hold on to the words.

Can't hold on to anything.

2

LEV

"Levka."

My eyes snap open to find Andrei loitering above me. I must have drifted off. Scrubbing a hand through my hair, I sit upright, my gaze drifting to the girl still sleeping on the sofa. Andrei is watching me watch her, and he is curious. This is never a good thing.

"Who is she?"

"Nobody," I answer sharply. Too sharply. The corner of Andrei's lip tips up, and he allows his gaze to roam the full length of her body as if it's a challenge. He can't really see anything beneath the blanket I draped over her, but he's irritating the fuck out of me, and he knows it. This is what Andrei wants. Everything is a challenge to him. From the day my uncle took me under his wing, my cousin has been a thorn in my side. He is jealous and petty, and everything becomes a competition with him.

"What do you need?" I stand and obstruct his view of Katerina.

"My father is on his way," he says. "He requested a meeting with both of us this afternoon."

A bitter taste coats my tongue as I offer him a stiff nod. There is no use arguing the matter. Whatever my uncle says is law. But I still suspect that Andrei didn't drag himself away from the bar just to tell me this news. He is curious about Katerina, as are all the other guys around the club. It is not common practice for me to bring a woman up here. Unlike Andrei, I don't make a habit out of fishing the easy pool of drunk women who frequent Delirium. I keep a low profile around here for a reason. As far as the rest of the Vory are concerned, I have no attachments. *Because attachments become vulnerabilities.*

I cross my arms and wait for Andrei to leave. He hesitates, considering some alternatives that might delay his departure. I can't be fucked dealing with him today, so I speed things along by reaching for my leather jacket and slipping it over my shoulders.

"I'm taking her home," I tell him. "What time does Vasily want to meet?"

"Noon," he grumbles.

"Then I will see you at noon."

With a grunt, he disappears into the elevator, and I am left alone with Katerina. I'm surprised when she peeks up at me from beneath the curtain of wild hair, and I wonder how much of the conversation she actually heard before she opened her eyes.

"Good morning," she offers in a raspy voice.

"Good morning." My eyes roam over her makeup-stained face. It looks as though she's had the night from hell, but somehow, she's still beautiful. Someone as young and pretty and vulnerable as her shouldn't be in a place like this. But she's only nineteen, I remind myself. Too young to know better. I wonder if she even remembers anything from last night. If she even realizes how badly her night could have ended if it had been someone else in my place. Tension floods my body as I allow myself to observe her; this tragic, wild creature who had the unfortunate luck of stumbling into my path. I can't decide what's worse, the monsters who tried to corner her last night, or the monster in me demanding that I allow myself just one taste. One kiss. One touch. One fuck.

Christ. She's staring up at me with those pale green eyes, and I'm becoming all too aware of the escalating temperature in the room. I need to look away. I need to be the one to grasp onto logical thought. Because right now, all I can think about is the way her body felt against mine when she was trying to climb me like a tree last night. If she remembers that, I can't tell, but when she clears her throat, I realize I need to fucking say something.

"There's a bottle of water." I gesture to the table. "And some Ibuprofen. I figured you might have a headache this morning."

I wait for her reaction, half expecting her to start demanding answers about what happened between us. But instead, she simply sits up and scrubs the sleep from her eyes before she reaches for the water. "Thank you for this. My throat is so dry."

"That's what happens when you party too hard," I observe, my tone harsher than I intend.

She winces and shakes her head, almost as if she's disappointed in herself. "I know. That was a really stupid thing to do."

"I won't disagree."

She glances up at me and frowns. I'm being an asshole, and I know it. Last night, she was practically begging me to fuck her. Pawing at me like I was her life raft. Now the illusion is shattered, and she's already looking for the nearest exit. I don't want to let her leave, but I need more than anything for her to go. For reasons I can't really comprehend in my current state of mind, I feel like a hunter staring at his prey. I'm drawn to this girl in a way I haven't been drawn to anyone else... ever. And that's exactly why I need to let her run, as fast and as far as she can.

"I'm sorry I took up so much of your time," she says. "I didn't mean to pass out. God, this is so embarrassing."

Words fail me when she glances at me nervously as she finger-combs her hair back into place and knots it at the nape of her neck with a hair tie. This entire encounter isn't something I'm particularly used to. I don't make a habit of small talk, and usually, if she was one of my hookups, I'd be long gone by now. But she isn't a hookup. Even though I can still feel her lips on mine, and I can still smell her arousal as she offered herself to me like a human sacrifice. My cock throbs at the memory, anxious to squeeze inside her and forget all the reasons this can't ever happen. I'm trying not to think about that when I point to her left.

"There's a bathroom if you need to use it."

"Oh, thank you," she murmurs as if I read her mind. She tosses the blanket aside and stretches, arching her back and displaying every curve in her body without being aware of it. In the light of day, her tight black pants and corset aren't doing anything to dull my senses.

She pads to the bathroom with bare feet, and I check my phone for any messages while I try to devise a plan. I need to take her home, drop her off, and tell her to have a nice life. That's the smart thing to do. But even as I tell myself that, I'm considering what I really want to do.

Katerina reappears from the bathroom, fresh-faced and slightly sheepish. She's scrubbed off her makeup, and now all that's left is her vulnerability. It shows when she slips back into the lace-clad gloves that cover the scar on the inside her forearm. The one I haven't been able to stop thinking about since I saw it.

Who hurt you?

I want to ask, but that's not a path I'm willing to go down. This girl, whoever she is, isn't for me. I don't do attachments. I don't rescue broken women. She needs a nice, sweet guy to set her straight and take her to dinner and the movies. That won't ever be me, and I already want to murder the motherfucker who gets to have those things with her.

"I'll take you home." I force the words out as she slips into her coat and boots.

"There's no need." She offers me a shy smile. "I already called Nina. She's coming to get me."

"Nina?" I repeat the name with obvious contempt, and it doesn't go unnoticed.

"Do you know her?" Katerina asks.

It isn't something I want to get into, so I deflect. "It's not a problem for me to drop you off."

Before she can reply, the elevator doors open, and Andrei appears again with a shit-eating grin on his face when he sees Katerina is awake. Motherfucker.

"My apologies, Levka. I didn't realize your friend was still here."

Sure, you didn't, asshole. "Did you need something else?"

"Yeah, I need to talk to you about those contracts."

"Right now?" I stare at him incredulously. He's getting on my last nerve this morning. He's like a fucking hound, sniffing out my every move. If he had his way, he'd be pissing circles around Kat right now too.

"We only have a short time before my father arrives," he answers. "I figured it's best to be prepared."

As much as I want to deny that he's right, the big oaf does have a point. The business we have to discuss isn't about any contracts, but it is time sensitive. When Vasily arrives today, I need to have my head in the game. But even knowing this, I'm still not ready to let Katerina run off just yet. It feels like we have unfinished business, but I don't yet know what it is. When I glance at her, she's already moving toward the elevator, slipping out of my grasp.

"I don't want to keep you," she says quietly. "I'll just let myself out. Nina's downstairs waiting for me."

I open my mouth to speak, but Andrei is watching me intently, and there is nothing I can say in his presence that he won't misread. So instead, I simply nod, and she offers me one last sad smile before the elevator doors close her in and sweep her away.

AFTER DISCUSSING the von Brandt family at length with Vasily, Andrei and I receive our marching orders. This job is not something I'm at all comfortable with, given my new association with Katerina. Though I don't particularly care for Nina, Kat considers her a friend. I can't help wondering how this might affect her if it goes south. But regardless, it's out of my hands.

William von Brandt brought this on himself, and whatever ill fate befalls him is his responsibility alone. Still, it does not sit easy with me as I consider the position he's put us in. Vasily does not give more than one warning. In many cases, he doesn't bother to give any. William is a father and a husband, and he's playing a dangerous game testing a Vor's patience this way.

I shake off those feelings and splash some cold

water onto my face as I stare at my reflection in the mirror. Sometimes, on days like today, I don't recognize the man staring back at me. What would my mother think if she could see me now? I close my eyes as a sharp pain lances through my chest. It's a pain that never goes away. No length of time or distance from her memory can spare me from this ache. She would certainly disapprove of my choices, but she isn't here to tell me so. She isn't here because someone took her from this world, and now the only recourse I have left is to find out who. At any cost. This is what keeps me going as I continue to show up and fall in line. Nothing can come between me and my revenge. *Her death cannot go unpunished.*

I shut the bathroom door behind me and consider heading down to the bar to dilute the blood in my veins with some good quality vodka. But before I get the opportunity, something on the sofa catches my eye. A piece of fabric peeks out from between the cushions, and I recognize it as the scarf Katerina was wearing last night. Sure enough, when I retrieve it and bring it to my nose, I can still smell her.

The beautiful, tragic woman continues to haunt me long after her absence. As I thread the fabric between my fingers, I wonder what it is about her that draws me in. She is exactly what I don't need in my life right now. Or ever, for that matter. Women are a vulnerability. But even as I consider it, I'm already making plans to return the scarf to her. Because now I'm curious about where she lives, and I need to see it for myself. I need to know that she made it home safely.

I stuff the scarf into my jacket and retrieve my phone as I head for the elevator. Pulling up the image of her license from last night, I type the address into my navigation app. It looks like she lives in an apartment complex about twenty minutes away. It's in the low-rent area of Philadelphia, which means it's also the highest crime district. Naturally, I have become well acquainted with these streets, but I can't imagine her living there.

Tightness lingers in my chest as some of the Vory brothers try to intercept me on my way out the door. The meeting has not been finished for more than thirty minutes, and already Andrei is displaying his drunken stupidity.

"Where are you off to so fast?" he demands.

"Good night, Andrei," I answer him dismissively.

He slips off his barstool in his attempt to stand and falls flat on his ass. Laughter erupts from the men around the bar, and I seize the moment of distraction to make a swift exit. Out on the street, I slip into my Audi and start the ignition, aiming the car for Katerina's apartment.

At least ten times during the drive, I consider

turning around. Or dropping the scarf in a mailbox. Perhaps leaving it in front of her door. I could handle this at least a dozen other ways without actually seeing her because I know if I see her, I won't be satisfied with simply giving her back the scarf. I'll ask her questions, and she'll become human to me. And then I will be royally fucked.

Regardless, the decision is made for me when I pull into the parking lot of the Shady Grove apartments. It's even more of a dump than I anticipated, and I think I must have entered the address incorrectly somehow. But one glance at the picture confirms that I'm in the right place. The decrepit brick building squatting on fractured concrete looks more suited to a prison than a residence. Several scrawny children kick a sun-bleached ball around the front courtyard, eyeing me curiously as I get out and shut the door behind me. They look at my car, and then my clothing before they skitter off into one of the complexes. I can't say that I blame them. If I saw me, I would run too.

I walk around the front and get a feel for the layout before I figure out Kat is in Building Two. Her apartment isn't difficult to find. It's on the ground level, and there's a sad-looking lawn chair and a wilted plant just outside the front door. At least she tried to decorate the place, I guess.

I hesitate at the door, considering whether I

should cross that threshold. I've already come this far, but it wouldn't be hard to dump the scarf in the chair and leave, never to look back. I know that's what I should do, but before I can force myself into action, a feminine voice startles me.

"What are you doing here?"

Turning, I find Katerina dressed in what appears to be a waitress uniform. She looks tired and nervous as her eyes drift to the scarf in my hands.

"Oh, thank God. I was looking everywhere for that."

She holds out her palm to retrieve it, but I hesitate, my eyes drifting down the length of her body. She notices, and a flush creeps over the delicate skin of her throat. I swallow, and tension swells between us like a bomb ready to detonate at any moment. Christ, what is it about this girl that makes me forget what the fuck I'm even doing here?

"Did you just get home from work?" I ask to break the silence.

She nods. "Yeah, I wait tables over at the diner on Fifth. It's nothing to write home about, but it pays the bills."

It doesn't look like it, but I don't tell her so.

The apartment door creaks open, and another woman who looks older than Kat pokes her head out. "Kat? I thought that was you. Everything okay out here?"

"Hey, Rachel." She waves at her friend. "I'm just talking to... uh..."

"Lev," I fill in the blank.

"Right." The blush on Kat's face deepens. "Lev was just returning my scarf."

"Okay." Rachel eyes me with curiosity before she eases the door closed. "See you in a few."

Kat nods, and the door shuts with an audible clunk. Silence lingers between us. I want to know what she's thinking, but as it turns out, I don't have to ask.

"I can't believe I never even asked your name," she blurts. "I'm so sorry if that came off as rude. But you just surprised me being here. How did you even find me, anyway?"

"Your driver's license," I remind her. "I went through your bag last night and confiscated the fake ID, remember?"

"Right." She rocks back on her heels. "And then you remembered my address and drove all the way over here to bring my scarf back?"

It sounds even creepier when she says it.

"I also thought you could use a meal," I offer lamely. "I wasn't in the best mood this morning, and I wanted to make up for it."

"Are you asking me to dinner?" Her eyebrows shoot up in surprise.

"Are you accepting?" A smile tugs at my lips, but I resist.

"Dinner would be nice, actually," she says. "I'm starving. Could you just give me two minutes to change?"

"Take your time." I plant myself in the rusty lawn chair. "I'll just be out here enjoying the view."

3

KAT

I'm not sure pink is still my favorite color, but I'm so happy Lev brought the scarf back. It's worn, the yarn coming apart in places, but I don't care. When I wear it, I feel safe.

"He's cute," Rachel says, waggling her eyebrows.

I pass her and head to my bedroom, trying to suppress my excitement. "I guess."

She follows me in. "You guess? I saw how you were looking at him. And how he was looking at you."

I can't help but smile when I turn to her again as I pull my uniform over my head.

"It's not like that. He's just being nice." I get a whiff of fried onion rings from the diner. It's probably in my hair too.

"Nice. Mm-hmm. Thought you said you spent the night at Nina's."

"Think I have time for a quick shower?"

"I can go keep him company if you like." She winks.

"Don't you dare." I hurry into our shared bathroom and push the curtain back to start the water. It always takes a few minutes to warm up.

"Tell me," she says, perching on the closed toilet seat as I rummage in my drawer for a razor.

"He just helped me last night. Nina had gotten me a little something special for my birthday, but well, it didn't go as planned."

Watching her face when I say it, I see it change as she grows more serious, and I instantly regret having told her that part.

"Kat—"

"It wasn't a big deal." I'm not in the mood for a lecture right now. "Everything turned out fine."

Stripping off my underwear, I step under the warm flow. I'm quick, shampooing once and working conditioner into my hair before shaving my legs. I didn't have time to shower before my shift at the diner, and between last night's escapades and today's various food smells, I stink.

Rachel pushes the curtain open just enough to peer inside.

"Hey, this is serious. You have to be careful. You

can't just buy something at a nightclub and expect to get what you think you're paying for. There are really bad people out there, Kat, and they will take advantage of you when you aren't in control of yourself."

"I know. It was stupid, but it turned out fine." Rachel is a recovering addict and doesn't have much patience for anything like this. "I didn't even like it if it makes any difference," I try, rinsing the conditioner out of my hair, forgetting to comb it out first in my hurry.

"Do you remember everything, then? The whole night?"

I shake my head even though I know I should lie and tell her I do.

She hands me a towel, and I wrap it around myself. She takes my hands, and I look at her.

"Be careful, Kat. It's not just the drugs. I mean, you don't even know this guy. Do you even know what happened after you passed out?"

I pull away. "Look, if he'd done anything, I'm pretty sure he wouldn't bother to drive all the way over here to bring me my scarf. And besides, I'd know if something like that happened."

"Not necessarily." She leans against the doorframe with her arms folded across her chest. She looks so much older than twenty-five, and although I don't know her whole story, I know enough.

I turn my attention to the meager offerings in my

closet and decide on a pair of jeans and a tight black long-sleeved T-shirt.

"Kat—"

"I'm not planning on doing it again, Rach. I promise." I hug her.

"Good. Because you got lucky once. That doesn't tend to repeat." She walks away, and I hate feeling as though I've disappointed her.

I run a wide-tooth comb through my hair, wincing when it catches on the tangles. I don't have time to dry it, so I squeeze as much moisture out of it as possible and tie it into a high ponytail, leaving a strand out on the right side of my face. He's already seen my arm. I don't need him to see the gash on my temple too.

After I apply mascara and lip gloss, I rummage through my jackets for a leather one. Well, it's pleather, but at least nothing had to die for it. Not that I'm vegan. I just don't have money to spend on luxuries.

I sit on the edge of the bed and consider the boots I wore last night. They're lying discarded in a corner of the room, but I can't imagine squeezing my feet into those after a nine-hour shift at the diner, so I reach for my worn and very comfortable Chucks and slide them on.

One final glance in the mirror and I wonder if

he's expecting me to look like I did last night. I don't. I never look that way, actually.

I remember what he said about my hair. I don't remember all the details, but some things I don't think I'll ever forget. At least I hope not to. He asked me why I dyed it when my natural color was so pretty. I'm a redhead, that golden-red that looks more girl-next-door than anything else. It's the same color as my mom's had been. But unlike her, I don't have too many freckles. Just three tiny ones scaling my right cheekbone in a neat little row and one on the very tip of my nose.

"You look great," Rachel says, coming back into the room.

I smile.

"Here." She holds out a small canister of what I know is pepper spray. "In case."

I sigh. Sometimes she's too much. "I don't need that, Rachel. I'll be fine."

"Just take it. It'll make me feel better."

I've been renting my room from Rachel for just under a year, and in all that time, I've never seen her go out on a date or bring anyone home.

"Fine." I take the canister. "But I won't need it."

"I hope you don't."

"See you."

I tuck the pepper spray into my purse, do a quick count of my cash—tips from today—and tuck my phone into my pocket. Picking up the scarf Lev returned, I head through the apartment to the front door and realize I'm nervous. I haven't been nervous, not like this, not that good kind of nervous, in a very long time.

I open the door and step out into the early evening. The fall air is crisp. He's watching the sunset, and I take a moment too. It's beautiful.

Lev stands up. He looks me over, and I'm hyperaware of how I look. And of how I don't look like I did last night.

"I didn't want to leave you sitting here while I dried my hair or put on makeup."

He cocks his head to the side and steps a little closer than what most people would consider comfortable. I smell him when he does that. Take in the scent of aftershave and remember how I'd liked his smell last night, too.

Tonight, though, it makes my mouth water.

"I like this better," he says.

I feel my face heat and bring my attention to wrapping my scarf around my neck.

"It's not cold enough for that, is it?" he asks.

I shrug a shoulder. "I just like to have it."

"Come on," he says, one big hand moving to my lower back as he guides me to his Audi. He even opens my door and waits for me to get in before walking around to the driver's side.

I take it all in. The sporty car, his leather jacket, his hair which he absently pushes off his face even though it falls right back down. I like it like that. He looks like a badass but cute too. And sexy.

It smells like him in here. Woodsy and clean and very masculine. The car itself is impeccably clean. I think if he saw my room, he'd flip.

"What do you feel like eating?" he asks as soon as he closes his door.

This is strange. We're going on a date. "Um, I don't mind. Italian? But anything's fine."

He nods and starts the car. "I know a place."

I look at him, wondering how he knows a place in my neighborhood, and then I wonder what he's waiting for. When he leans over me and he's so close, I think he's going to kiss me. I lick my lips, staring into his chocolate eyes, but nothing happens. Well, a corner of his mouth curves upward into a one-sided grin, and his eyes narrow a little as though he knows just what I'm thinking. I wonder how old he is. How experienced. If he works at the club, he must meet girls all the time. He must take girls upstairs all the time.

I feel my face flush with heat, and that one-sided grin widens to spread across his face. He knows exactly what he's doing as he reaches for my seat belt and drags it across my chest, his face still inches from mine, hand not quite touching me but close enough that I swear electricity sparks between us.

"Safety first," he says with a wink. His gaze slides downward momentarily before he's back in his seat and shifting the car into first.

I touch my face. It feels hot. I adjust my shirt because what he was looking at were my nipples trying to tear through the fabric in anticipation of our kiss.

"Safety first," I repeat. Can he hear my disappointment at the non-kiss?

He pulls expertly out of the parking lot, driving fast but fully in control of the sporty Audi. I watch as his big hand shifts gears seamlessly, merging with traffic, his body relaxed, casual as he glances at me, then back at the road.

In profile, he's not so much cute anymore as hyper-masculine and very sexy. It's his jawline, chiseled and hard and with that perfect five o'clock shadow.

"What are you looking at?" he asks me.

I snap my gaze straight ahead, embarrassed and still nervous. I've never really dated. Well, a few times since I moved in with Rachel but no one like Lev. No one I ever felt this way around.

I turn to him. "Why did you come all the way out here to bring me my scarf?"

He glances at me momentarily, dark eyes clear.

There's something wild inside them. Something carnal.

He licks his lips before he answers, and when he swallows, I watch his Adam's apple work. Can a man's Adam's apple be sexy?

Something is seriously wrong with me.

"I wanted to see you again," he says, and it's what I want to hear. "Tell me your story, Katerina Blake."

I'm taken aback, wondering how he knows my last name. But then I remember he'd taken a photo of my driver's license. The real one. That was how he found me in the first place.

"I don't know your last name," I say.

"It's Antonov," he answers shortly after turning his attention back to the road.

"Where are you from?"

"I asked your story first."

"I'm pretty sure yours will be more interesting than mine." Never mind the fact that I don't like to tell mine. It's not a pretty one.

"Tell me and I'll let you know."

"Okay." Here goes. "I've lived here since I was a toddler. I mean, not here in the apartment but in the area, mostly just outside Philadelphia. Graduated high school last year and have been on my own since. I go to night school at the local community college in addition to working at the diner." CliffsNotes version. "See, boring."

"What do you study?" he asks.

We're in the city now, and he's taking a turn onto South 2nd Street. I wonder where he's taking me. I rarely get to this part of the city although I love it.

"I want to become a teacher. You know, work with kids. Help them."

He gives me a look like he's surprised and pleased at once. "And your family? Your background? I thought Eastern European."

"Why did you think that?"

"Bone structure. But then your eyes and hair made me think Irish?"

I'm surprised. "My mom was Irish. No one ever notices, I think."

"Then they're not paying attention. We're here," he announces as he snags a tight spot between two parked cars on a side street off South 2nd.

I look around but don't see much. "Where are we going?"

"Giacomo's," he says, climbing out of the car and closing his door.

I'm just undoing my seat belt when he unexpectedly opens my door and holds out his hand.

I'm...surprised. He's a gentleman.

Placing my hand in his, I let him help me out. He locks the doors, drops his keys into the pocket of his jeans, and with a hand at my back, he guides me around the corner to a tiny place that I would probably not look twice at. But when he opens the door and I smell the delicious smells of Italian, my stomach growls. I'm just glad it's noisy and hope he doesn't hear it.

"Only Italians. And us," he says.

He nods to someone, an older man who smiles widely and gestures to the only empty table in the place. I walk ahead of him, weaving through the closely situated round tables, and take a seat in the one the older man pulls out for me, liking the casual place, the red and white checkered tablecloth and rickety table and chairs. A candle burns in the heavily waxed-over Chianti bottle on the table and the kitchen opens onto the restaurant so I can see the cook.

"It's old-fashioned, but the food is delicious. I hope you like it."

"It's great and smells wonderful. We're near Elfreth's Alley, right?"

"Yep. You like it there?"

"Yeah. I like walking around there when I have the time."

The older man who'd smiled to Lev comes over, and they shake hands. He gives us two menus. Lev orders a bottle of wine, then turns to me. "Red okay? I know you're underage, but..." he trails off purposely, and I know he's taking a dig at me.

"Red's great," I say as the man leaves. "And can I have the ID back that you took from me last night?"

"No, you cannot," he says, reaching to take my menu.

"I haven't even looked at it yet," I say.

"Do you read Italian?"

I glance down and see the laminated but still worn-out menu is in Italian. "Oh."

"You like gnocchi?" he asks.

"I love it."

The man returns with the wine, opens the bottle, and pours two glasses. Lev orders for us and picks up his glass. He waits for me to do the same.

"To seeing you again in one piece and able to talk and walk on your own," he says.

My smile vanishes, and I put my glass down. "Are you just going to lecture me about last night? Because if you are, then..." I trail off, because then what? I'll take a taxi home? I don't want to leave.

He reaches over to put his hand over mine. "Relax. I'm not going to lecture you, but I am going to tell you that it was a pretty stupid thing to do buying that shit off someone you don't know."

My shoulders slump, and I pull my hand out from under his.

His smile is gone, and although he doesn't look angry, his eyes are harder, like they got a few times last night.

"Not to mention letting me take you upstairs when you were in that state. Another man may have taken advantage. They might have hurt you, Katerina."

"All right, I'm done." I move to stand, but he closes his hand over my knee. I look down. It's so big it covers the whole of it, wrapping almost entirely around it.

"Stay," he says, the single syllable a quietly spoken command.

Something stirs in my belly, but I don't let myself think about that. Instead, I glare because I get the feeling I don't have a choice.

"You need to be careful, especially at a place like Delirium. Don't come back there, got it?"

"Don't worry, I won't now that I know I'm not welcome."

He pulls his hand back and leans toward me. "It's not that you're not welcome. It's just not…safe. You don't belong there—"

"I don't belong there?" I should feel angry. I wish I felt angry, but I just feel hurt. My shoulders cave, and I hug my arms around my middle, sliding the one underneath the sleeve of my shirt to that spot, scratching at the bumpy skin, wincing when I reopen a cut.

"Don't you remember what I told you last night?" he asks more gently.

I search his eyes, looking for a sign that he's mocking me, but he doesn't seem cruel. Doesn't seem angry even.

"What does your name mean?" he continues when I don't answer.

I draw my hand out from under my sleeve, wipe the little bit of blood on my already red napkin, and pick up my glass. I pretend to take a sip because I can't swallow right now.

"Katerina means pure. That place isn't good, and I'm not usually there, Kat."

I feel like he's warning me.

"Do you understand?" he asks.

"Nina knew you." I remember suddenly.

His expression doesn't change, but his eyes close off a little.

"So, who are you?" I continue.

"Her father does some work for my uncle."

"Who's your uncle?" My mind is making up scenarios, that Russian accent suddenly much more prominent.

Our food arrives then, and Lev smiles up at the old man who keeps talking in Italian. A plate of gnocchi topped with red sauce is placed in front of each of us, and a moment later, he's gone.

It looks delicious and smells even better. I haven't eaten all day, and even given the uncomfortable situation, I'm starving.

When he leaves, I look up to find Lev's eyes still on me. "Do you speak Italian too?"

"Too?"

"I heard you talking with your friend—"

"He's not my friend," he cuts me off, his expression hardening. "I was born in Moscow. Lived in the States most of my life, though and no, I don't speak Italian, but I do understand some. Giacomo was saying that he finds you beautiful and to enjoy our meal." His expression softens again, and he tries for a smile. "Lecture over, Kat. Now to the business of why I returned your scarf."

"Because you wanted to see me again." Am I stupid that the thought makes me feel warm inside? Makes me feel good?

He puts a forkful of gnocchi into his mouth and smiles wide. His expression and the little bit of red sauce on the corner of his mouth make me smile, too.

4

LEV

A soft glow blooms across Katerina's cheeks as the evening wears on, and I can't tell if it's the wine, the candlelight, or me. She's loosening up, telling me bits and pieces about her life. Her friends. Her living situation. Her work. These are details I wouldn't typically care to know about anyone else, but with her, I've barely scratched the surface.

I want to know about her scars. Her pain. Every tear she's ever shed and every secret that might pour from those lips. And worse yet, I want to know what she'd look like coming around my cock. Does she have freckles everywhere? Is her entire body as soft as her hands?

Christ. It's been far too long since I've felt the warmth of a woman in my bed. This isn't the one I should break that dry spell with because I'm already in too deep. But I can't stop staring at her. Soaking her in. Inhaling her scent every time she moves and leans a little closer.

Before I realize it, Giacomo is asking if there's anything else I need before he sends the staff home for the night. A glance around the restaurant proves that we've been here for hours. All the other guests have gone, and I failed to notice.

I thank Giacomo and give him an extra tip for his service before pulling out Kat's chair and helping her into her coat. She looks a little crestfallen that the evening is coming to an end, and I'm tempted to tell her that it's not. But as I walk her to the car and open her door, I know that taking her home is the right thing to do. I did what I came to do. I returned her scarf, and I made sure she was safe. There can't be anything more to it than that. But when I sink into the driver's seat and glance over at her, she smiles at me in challenge.

She hasn't buckled her seat belt, and we're playing a dangerous game. I lean into her again, dragging the belt across her thighs and tucking it into place. She shivers when my fingers brush against her arm, and I make the fatal mistake of glancing up at her. Her eyes are the softest shade of green I've ever seen. They seem to change with the light, and right now the deep ring of blue around the edges is vibrating with a want she can't deny.

I'm not thinking clearly when my thumb grazes over her lips. It's second nature to want to experience her this way. Kat sucks in a breath. Our eyes lock, and for a minute, all of my problems cease to exist. She grabs me again, like she did last night, and this time, I don't fight her. My mouth crashes into hers as my fingers fall to the beating pulse in her throat. Katerina arches into me, dragging her fingers through my hair as she moans into my mouth. She's a goddamn wildfire, and I can't put her out.

"Katya," I murmur against her lips. "You are so much fucking trouble for me."

She blinks and pulls away, just enough to look up at me. "Katya?"

I smooth her hair back into place and sigh. I'm revealing too much of myself. Getting too familiar with her. I should lie, but I would demand honesty of her, so I can only give her the same. "It is another way of saying your name in Russian. Like a nickname."

"Katya," she repeats. "Will you say it again with your accent?"

She snares her lip between her teeth, and I bite back a groan as I consider her doing the same when I sink inside her. When I finally manage to speak again, my voice is rougher than I've ever heard it.

"I should take you home."

"You could," she answers hesitantly. "Or you could take me back to your place."

"Christ." I lean back against my own seat, trying to gather my thoughts. "You're killing me here."

"This doesn't have to be a hard decision," she says softly. "You're hot, and I like you. And I think you like me, right? So, forget about all the rest. Let's just focus on tonight."

I open my eyes and glance over at her. My dick is uncomfortably hard. I know if I were to slide my fingers between her thighs, she would be wet for me. It isn't smart or logical, but perhaps, she is right. For tonight only, I can indulge this fixation I have with her, and tomorrow, I will say goodbye to her for good.

"Fuck it." I start the ignition and shift the car into gear.

"Is that a Russian yes?" She laughs softly.

I glance over at her with a smirk. "That's a Russian yes."

Despite the levity in my voice, tension returns to my body as I navigate the familiar streets back to my rental in the unsuspecting neighborhood of Chestnut Hill. I've never brought a woman back to my place before. But I'm not about to suggest a hotel, and Kat's apartment is out of the question with her roommate there.

She is quiet as she watches the scenery outside the windows change from her familiar stomping grounds to mine. I don't know what she's thinking, but I can only imagine this will inevitably invite more questions. Questions I can't answer.

"You never told me what you did for a living."

My jaw flexes, and I think I hate this question more than anything. "I do odd jobs."

"Like what?" she presses.

I glance at her as the car comes to a stop in my driveway. "I can't tell you the things I do, Kat. That's the deal, and it's something I can't negotiate on. If you want to back out now, it's not too late for me to take you home."

She frowns as her gaze moves to the one-bedroom stone cottage beneath the tree canopy that this area is known for. It doesn't look threatening, and it's not. Nobody but my uncle knows I live here, and I've been content to keep it that way, until her.

"I guess I just have one question then." She folds her hands into her lap, obscuring the scars as she often does without thinking about it. "Can I trust you?"

It would be a lie to give her an unequivocal yes, but I suspect she already knows that. Intentions are only as good as the moments they are spoken in, and those moments are often fleeting. I have a feeling Katerina understands that better than most.

"You are safe with me tonight," I tell her. "What happens now is up to you."

Her shoulders relax, and she lets out a shaky laugh. "Then I want to go inside. Show me your world, Lev."

I shudder at her choice of words, relieved she could never understand the full weight of her request. The only part of my world she can ever see is this small space where I sleep at night. This is all that can ever be ours, and it's a limited-time offer.

After shutting off the car, I walk around to open her door and help her out. The gravel crunches beneath our shoes as we walk to the front door, and I can feel her sudden nerves as I turn the key in the lock. When the door opens, I gesture inside for her to enter first. It needs to be her decision. She was brave back in the car, but I don't know that she will remain that way.

Once the lights are on and she can see the space for herself, it doesn't take her long to relax. I take her coat, and she tests out the sofa while I drop my keys and wallet in the kitchen.

"Would you like anything to drink?" I offer.

"No thanks," she says. "Did you choose this furniture yourself?"

I meet her gaze with a smirk. "Does it look like I did?"

She eyeballs the neutral tones and pieces that

seem to fit together naturally. "Not really. Doesn't seem like your style."

"It came with the rental," I tell her. "I wanted something that was move-in ready. It's just more convenient."

I leave out the part that I intentionally chose a place I could leave behind in a hurry if it ever came to it. Clothes, furniture, cars... these things are all disposable in my line of work. They have to be. The only thing of value I've ever kept is the metalwork my father and I used to work on together in his shop. And when it comes down to it, that's the only thing in this house I'd ever need to take with me.

Kat nods as if my explanation clears up her own suspicions as I flip on the gas fireplace and kick off my shoes. I take a seat beside her on the sofa, and without thinking about it, my arm comes to rest around her shoulder. Kat leans into me like it's the most natural thing in the world, and it chokes some of the air from my lungs.

I can't keep her.

She turns to me and looks up, and I know what she wants. But if I only have tonight with her, I intend to take my time. I want to experience every inch of her, with nothing left on the table.

"Kat."

"Hmm?" she murmurs, eyes soft and warm.

"You are so fucking beautiful. You don't even realize it, do you?"

My words light the match to the slow-burning flame inside her, and her response is to crawl onto my lap and grasp my face in her palms. I groan as my lips collide with hers, and my hands come to rest on her hips. She rocks her pelvis against my swollen dick, arching her body into mine, and it's the most erotic thing I've ever seen.

Her hair is a mess from my hands. But right now, she's mine. My tongue slips between her lips, and our teeth clash as the hunger in my veins demands more.

Kat peels off my coat as I kiss my way down the sensitive flesh of her throat. She shivers for me, so alive, so responsive, and I know I'm already half done for. When I get inside her, once isn't going to be enough. I have every intention of fucking her until the sun comes up, and I tell her as much when I reach for the hem of her shirt.

She responds in kind, frantic, scrambling to eliminate the obstacles between us. At some point, she removes my belt, and then I get her shirt off. She unclasps her bra and tosses it aside, and I freeze.

"What?" She glances down in panic as though I'm seeing something I shouldn't.

Before she can get too much in her head, I dip forward and suck her nipple between my teeth and then release it before moving to the other side. Her fingers thread through my hair, digging into my skull as she arches into me. She cries out when I tug on her jeans, loosening them enough to slip my hand into the cotton band of her panties.

"Lev!" She squirms as I make contact with her swollen clit, soaked with want for me.

I toy with her slowly, building her up and then backing off as I rub her beautiful tits against my face. It's torturous and not just for her. I want to feel her body wrapped around mine, but not until she comes for me at least once. It won't take much. I can feel it in the tightening of her muscles and the hiss of her breath every time I stop. Before she even realizes it, she's pleading with me, gasping stuttered words between breaths as she begs me to free her.

I flip her onto her back, tugging her jeans and panties off and pausing to admire her one more time. She's completely naked, and she's never looked so vulnerable... or so sweet. My dick throbs when I realize that I was right about her freckles. She does have a few more scattered across her creamy skin. I want to connect all the dots with my tongue and devour her like the wolf she thinks I am right now.

"Spread your legs for me," I command.

She does as I ask, her eyes never leaving mine as I position myself between her thighs. I kiss my way up the delicate expanse of skin until she's a writhing, panting mess.

"Oh my God, Lev... please."

Her words fall short when I bury my face between her legs and eat her like she's my dessert. Katerina rewards me with everything I want to hear. Her body quivers and tenses as she claws at my back and mumbles incoherently. There is no coming back this time. She's too far gone, and I only realize it when she spasms around my tongue and cries out in agony.

The orgasm seems to go on forever, scorching her every nerve and completely wrecking her. When she finally opens her eyes again, she is breathless and exhausted, but she understands what I need from her.

"Don't stop," she whispers. "Don't ever stop."

There isn't time to think about it. I'm acting on autopilot when I tug down my briefs and drag my aching cock against her wetness. I close my eyes, and she digs her fingers into the base of my spine as I sink into her warmth. *Pure. Fucking. Heaven.*

I sigh and then thrust, and she wraps her legs around me, pulling me deeper into her body. Our mouths come together in another frenzy, and I fuck her into the couch, my own agony escaping between our lips.

We've run out of words. I have no need for them.

I just need to keep fucking her like this until I have nothing left. And that's what I do. I thrust into her over and over again, driving myself to the brink. There's a small, nagging voice in the back of my mind that I need to stop before it goes too far. But before I can think it through, Katerina leans up and drags her teeth down my throat. That feeling travels straight down my spine and explodes into my dick. I'm not thinking straight when I bury myself inside her with a grunt, releasing what feels like a metric ton of pressure from my balls.

Fuck.

I blink and look down at her, and I think she knows we fucked up too, but neither of us can acknowledge it. Or at least that's what I believe ... until she speaks.

"It's okay."

I collapse into her and wonder how she knows it's okay. Is she on birth control? I can't voice my concerns. But she must be if she's giving me her assurances, right? The alternative is too terrifying to imagine, so I let myself believe her. I'm still inside her, and she isn't asking me to get off. So, I kiss her. I kiss the hell out of her. And pretty soon, that kiss evolves into something else, reigniting a need I never knew I had. I take her two more times before the sun comes up, and we finally collapse into a coma in front of the fire.

At some point during the night, my body curls around hers, and she sighs against me as though it's exactly what she needs. It feels right, but I know everything will change when we wake again. My suspicions prove correct when I hear her mumbling something in her sleep, and it pulls me back to consciousness.

Her expression is pained, and it looks like a war is raging in her head as she murmurs the name again.

"Joshua." Her body tenses, and it's obvious she's having a nightmare, but all I can think about is who the fuck Joshua is.

I watch her for several minutes, waiting for it to pass, but it never does. That's when I notice another scar on her temple. I hadn't seen it before because of her hair, and it feels like another secret. This girl has proven to be full of them. When she jerks awake, she catches me staring, and the resulting shame is written all over her face. She drags a handful of hair down to obscure the scar, and I can't figure out why it bothers me so much. Last night she was open for me, and today, she is closed.

"You were having a nightmare," I observe.

"I was?" She blinks.

"Who is Joshua?" I ask before I can think about all the reasons I shouldn't.

In a split second, Katerina shuts the question down with a shake of her head. "Nobody."

Nobody. It doesn't feel like nobody as she scrambles to her feet and grabs her clothes.

"I need to use the bathroom," she says.

I nod, and she disappears down the hall as I stumble to my feet and find my jeans. She's lying to me, and if there's one thing I can't stand, it's dishonesty. But then I remind myself it's none of my goddamned business. That was the plan, right?

In the light of day, everything is clear again. I don't know this girl. Not really. And I can't afford to get to know her. However those scars came to be, I can't fix that for her. I can't slay her demons when I have my own. The best thing I can do for both of us is take her home and tell her goodbye. That's the only logical conclusion. Every other path is a recipe for disaster.

I'm no good for her, and she's definitely no good for me. Not with the type of life I lead. Her absence serves as a reminder of that, and by the time she's returned, she notices the cold front when she finds me in the kitchen.

"You have somewhere you need to be?" she asks, noting that I've put on my jeans.

"I'll make you some breakfast," I tell her. "And then I'll take you home."

5

KAT

I wrap my scarf around my neck as I take a seat at his kitchen table.

"You cold?"

I try for a smile that doesn't quite work and shake my head. "Just don't want to forget it again," I say as I pick up the mug of black coffee he puts in front of me. He doesn't sit down.

He's different this morning. Distant. Not quite cold but not really here either.

"I can catch a bus—"

"I'll take you home after you eat," he cuts me off with barely a glance over his shoulder.

"You seem busy, that's all."

He doesn't reply. I watch his back as he works and remember last night. Remember how he was at dinner. Remember how he was after. My belly does a little flip, but a moment later, my heart sinks.

He doesn't want me here, but he's being polite.

"Here," Lev says, setting a plate of scrambled eggs in front of me.

I'm not hungry, but I set my mug down and pick up my fork.

He doesn't quite meet my eyes as he pulls out his chair after setting his own plate down. I'm about to open my mouth—to ask if something happened or if I did something—

when his phone rings.

Abandoning his breakfast, he goes to the counter and looks at the display. He mutters what I'm sure is a curse in Russian under his breath and picks up the phone. Turning his back to me, he walks into the living room and answers the call.

I eat a bite of the eggs but taste nothing.

He speaks in Russian to whoever is on the phone, and he sounds angry. But maybe that's just how Russian sounds. Or maybe Lev isn't a morning person.

When he raises his voice just before disconnecting the call, I focus on my plate, listening as he returns to the table. He doesn't sit down but takes his still full plate and dumps the uneaten breakfast into the trashcan.

I cram another forkful into my mouth, cover

what I haven't eaten with a napkin, and follow his lead to empty my plate, but he catches my wrist before I turn it over.

"You didn't eat," he says.

His grip is harder than it needs to be, like he's still angry from that call.

I look down at where he's holding me, see the difference between us. See how big his hand is and how easily he could snap my wrist if he wanted to.

My mind races to last night, to how he gripped my knee the same way at the restaurant. What had he said he did? Odd jobs for his uncle? I didn't think much of it then—probably due to the wine, not to mention my hormones going crazy around him.

No hormones to muddle my thoughts this morning, though.

This morning, he's just scary.

It seems like an eternity passes as these thoughts race through my head, but I know it's just seconds, and when I turn my gaze up to his, he lifts his too.

I bite the inside of my cheek as I stare into his now almost black eyes.

Clearing his throat, he releases my wrist and takes a step backward.

I can breathe again and turn my attention to clearing off my dish, then place it on top of his in the sink.

"Ready?" he asks, his voice tight as he picks up his keys.

"Ready," I say, slipping on my jacket and picking up my purse, remembering the pepper spray Rachel had given me. Not that I think I'll have to use it, but Lev is different this morning.

He opens the front door and gestures for me to step out. It's a gray morning with a light drizzle falling. I hate rain, and when it comes, I wish it would rain hard and get it over with, then move on, but some of these gray days seem to melt into whole weeks, especially this time of year.

Lev opens the passenger door, and I get in. This time, I don't wait for him to strap me in but do it myself.

He glances over at me when he settles into the driver's seat and nods his approval, then starts the car, and we begin the tense drive to my house.

"I really can take the bus," I try again when his phone dings with a text message that he quickly glances at before setting it facedown on the console.

"I'm sure you can, but you won't." He keeps his gaze straight out the window.

I look straight ahead too, gritting my teeth. "I don't like feeling like a burden. I'm capable of taking care of myself." I pause. "And you clearly have somewhere else you'd rather be," I add a moment later.

He snorts, and I glance over to see him give a

shake of his head as he shifts his gaze to me, a smile or a sneer on his face.

"You're not a burden. I just have some shit I have to take care of." He schools his features, and it's silent again for a long moment. "Who's Joshua?" he asks again, taking me by surprise.

Our eyes meet for a split second, and in that instant, I see Lev like he was last night.

I turn to look out my window as I tug my scarf closer even though it's warm in the car.

"You called out his name in your sleep."

Shit.

"Twice."

He slows the car as we hit rush-hour traffic.

Taking a deep breath, I slip my hand beneath my shirt sleeve and rub the skin there. I turn back to find Lev's eyes on me.

"Just a friend I used to know."

"Past tense?"

I haven't talked about Joshua in two years. I haven't said his name out loud to anyone, not even to myself. I don't remember the dream, but I can guess what it was. And it'd be more in the category of nightmare.

A weight settles across my chest like a strap being tightened around me. My jaw tightens too, and I feel my face harden. My eyes go cold.

"He's dead. So yeah, past tense. As past tense as you can get."

He studies me, but I can't read if he's surprised or what.

Traffic crawls, and I watch the light change from yellow to red. Someone honks their horn, and Lev opens his mouth to say something or maybe to ask me another question about Joshua when he's being kind of a dick after last night, but I don't wait to find out. Instead, as soon as the car comes to a stop, I simultaneously push the button to unlatch my seat belt and open the door. I have one leg out, and before he can say a word, I turn to him.

"It'll be faster if I walk from here. I know a shortcut."

"Hey." He reaches over, and I just slip out before he can grab my arm.

I lean down as the light turns green, and the car behind us honks its horn. "Thanks for dinner and the ride." I slam the door shut and sprint through three lanes of traffic, not looking back until I'm on the sidewalk and ducking around a corner and out of sight.

I stop there, hugging my jacket to myself. The zipper's broken so I can't close it, but I take cover from the rain that seems to have picked up as soon as I got out of the car under the overhang of a closed shop. I take in big gulps of air and scrub my face with my hands as my heart races.

My head hurts. Probably the wine and lack of sleep. I push off the wall. There's no shortcut, but there is a bus. Although it's not a direct route, so it'll take me a good forty-five minutes to get home. I need to get moving so I duck my head against the rain and start doing just that because it's what I do. I go on. I survive.

Last night was amazing.

Last night, I felt something I never thought I'd feel. I'm going to chalk that up to not having had sex in too long. And sex with Lev, well, I'll miss that because I know I won't see him again, and even as I try to shut my brain up, I know it's more than that. I liked him. It's stupid, but I did. And maybe what's pathetic about it is that it wasn't just the sex or that he looks like he does or any of that. It's that he seemed genuine and nice. Like he really cared about me.

"Fuck."

I shake my head and snort. I'm an idiot.

I liked him because he was nice to me. Pathetic.

Wiping what I want to say is rain from my eyes, I dig my phone out of my purse and text Nina.

Me: Hey. You there?

Nothing. But I'm not surprised. It's early, and Nina doesn't do mornings.

Me: You knew the guy at the club the other night. Lev Antonov. Who is he?

I hit send and tuck the phone into my back pocket just as the bus turns the corner. I run the last half-block to make it. But just before I get to the stop, I see the little black Audi turn the same corner the bus just turned and I stand, my mouth falling open as Lev easily overtakes the slower bus and pulls up in front of the shelter.

He opens the driver's side door and gets out, and he looks pissed off.

The bus honks its horn as it approaches the stop, making me jump, but Lev ignores it. We're only a few feet apart, and rain is coming down in sheets now, soaking us both as we stare at each other.

"Get in," Lev orders.

I open my mouth, gesture to the bus, but before I can utter a word, he stalks around the car, takes my arm, and forces me to the Audi.

"I said get the fuck in," he repeats, voice icing my spine as he deposits me roughly into the passenger seat.

As if suspecting I might try to make a run for it, he clicks the lock on the door as he makes his way around to the driver's side, the bus a hulking, angry shadow behind us as a soaking wet Lev gets in behind the wheel and shifts into gear. He speeds off so fast, I scream when we swerve on the slippery road.

I don't expect him to actually stop at the stop sign, but he does and turns to me. I know why a moment later when he angrily draws the belt across my lap and clicks it into place.

"I told you I'd take you home," he says through gritted teeth.

I press my back into the seat. He's so close, I feel his breath on my face, smell his smell that still does something to me.

A moment later, he's speeding to my house, seeming to know every street and every alley. The car moves fast, swerving around the slower vehicles and pissing off more people than I can count.

I reach into my purse and wrap my hand around the pepper spray, and when we get to my apartment building, I'm not sure what to do.

He parks the car at the curb, not in a parking space but just right there. I clear my throat, hand still around that canister as I reach with the other to open my door. My heart is racing, has been during the entire time of this second drive.

But before I can open my door, he's out and around the car and opens my door for me. He wraps a hand around my arm to pull me out.

"I'm coming," I try as I stumble out, my purse

falling off my lap, my wallet and keys spilling to the ground.

He doesn't look at those things though. His gaze is on the pepper spray. When he meets my eyes, which I'm sure are like those of a deer in headlights, he just snorts, shakes his head and closes his giant hand around my wrist, then releases my arm to use that hand to pry the pepper spray from me.

"Smart to have that," he says. "You should always have pepper spray. You never know when you'll need it," he adds, keeping hold of my wrist as he bends to pick up my fallen purse and keys. He drops the canister into my bag and walks me to the door.

"Roommate home?"

I shake my head, knowing Rachel is at work.

Using my key, he unlocks the door and walks me inside. He stands there a moment and looks around, and I see it how he must see it. Small and ugly and a little sad.

"Your room?"

"Uh..."

He tugs me to him, holding my wrist at a painful angle. "Your room," he repeats.

"Last one." I point down the hall.

He walks toward it, and I follow because I have no choice. He opens my bedroom door, and we step inside. He closes it, and once again, he stops, taking in the messy space. The unmade bed. The clothes strewn over the back of a chair and on the floor.

"You're a mess," he says.

"Lev?"

He walks me into the bathroom, eyes the other door of the shared space and locks it from the inside.

I sneeze, suddenly shivering.

"Get undressed," he says. "You're going to catch a cold."

He still has hold of my wrist as he pushes the shower curtain back and runs the water, testing the temperature before shifting the flow to the shower.

When he turns back to me and sees I'm still dressed, he raises his eyebrows.

"My hand," I say, my voice trembling.

He nods, releases it, and watches as I peel off my jacket, drop it to the ground, then my shirt, which is soaked through. I drop that too, but when it comes to undoing my jeans, my hands are too shaky to unbutton them.

"Christ," he says, gripping the waistband of my jeans and tugging me to him, and I realize again how much bigger than me he is. Taller and so much stronger.

His eyes are almost black again, and I see the hunger and desire I saw last night. He holds my gaze as he undoes my jeans, and with his other hand, he grabs the back of my head and pulls me to him. His mouth, wet with rain, on mine, kisses me with a fierce hunger as he unzips my jeans.

I make a sound, wanting him again. I'm turned on by this violence, which I know is sick and wrong, but it's how I'm wired. How I learned sex is.

And so, when he grips my hair and pulls my head back, I'm panting, and I want more.

He spins me around, putting my hands on the edge of the sink.

"Don't move." He gets behind me so I can see him in the mirror. He pushes the hair off my neck and kisses my thudding pulse, then bites just hard enough to hurt as he slides one hand inside my jeans and panties and cups my sex.

I moan with the contact, his fingers roughly kneading my clit, rougher than he was last night.

"Lev." I turn my head to kiss him.

He tugs my wet jeans down over my hips and pushes me forward a little. I look at him looking down at me, then feel a hard smack.

I gasp, meeting his black eyes in the mirror.

"I should have spanked your ass for the night at the club, but I thought I gave you enough of a scare at the restaurant."

He smacks me again three quick slaps to the same spot. The sting is sharp and does more to turn me on than punish me. He grins, raking his fingernails over my ass.

"You like this, Kat?" He spanks me again. "If I'd known..."

I hear the zipper of his jeans, and a moment later, I feel his length at my back.

"Watch. I want to see your eyes when I fuck you."

I turn to the mirror as he spreads my ass open, and I moan at the length of him as he rubs himself through my folds.

"Fuck." He sucks in a breath, and I'm panting. When I lean forward, he grips a handful of hair and tugs my head up. "I said I want to see your eyes when I fuck you."

He pushes into me then. I'm still sore from last night, but he feels even bigger than last night, and I can't get enough of him.

"I like fucking your tight little cunt, Katerina. I like coming inside your wet little cunt."

He's squeezing my ass cheek in one hand and pulling my hair with the other, and fuck, I want to come.

I slip my hand from the lip of the sink and slide it between my legs, and Lev grins a wicked grin.

"And that's your punishment for this morning," he says, smacking my ass one more time before taking my hand and pressing it back to the counter, trapping it as he fucks me hard. He grunts with each thrust, his cock so deep I swear I can feel it in my belly.

"I need..." I try to pull my hand free, but he laughs.

"You need to come, but you're not going to." His thrusts come faster, and I feel him thickening inside me. "You get to watch me come instead."

Fuck.

My God. Fuck.

"Please!" I cry out, but his grip only tightens in my hair. He tilts my head to the side, and when he closes his mouth over my throat and stills inside me, I feel him throb, feel him empty. I watch his face, his beautiful, wicked face as he takes his fill of me, and I think I hate him and I love him at once. I want him. I want more of him. Him inside me like this.

When he's finished, he blinks his eyes, then draws his head back.

He looks at the smear of red at my pulse and licks the spot he's just been biting hard enough to break the skin. He lets go of my hair and holds both of my wrists behind my back as he pulls out of me.

I feel the gush of warmth as cum slides down my thighs, and I smell us. I smell sex and want, and I smell my own hunger. My need.

He leans in close to my ear. "Get in the shower and keep your hands off your pussy."

When he lets go of my wrists and steps away, I have to grip the counter to stay upright.

He tucks himself back into his jeans and zips up.

I turn to him.

"You're wasting water, Kat." He gestures to the shower, wipes something from the corner of his mouth with his thumb, then folds his arms across his chest and leans against the wall.

I move to strip off my jeans, embarrassed as he watches me, embarrassed at the smear of wet on the insides of my thighs. I step into the shower and go to pull the curtain closed, but he shakes his head.

"Nuh-uh. I want to watch. Make sure you don't get yourself off when you wash my cum off you."

Fuck.

I wash myself, embarrassed again, but also turned on.

He checks his phone. I don't know if it's a message, or he's just checking the time. He did seem like he was in an awful rush this morning. He tucks his phone into his back pocket.

"That's good enough," he says, reaching in to switch off the water. He looks around for a towel, grabs one, and unfolds it.

I step out and let him wrap me in it. Let him dry me.

He walks me into my bedroom. "Get dressed before you get cold."

I open a dresser drawer, then pull on panties, a pair of yoga pants, and a sweater. I don't bother with a bra.

Lev is standing across the room, looking at something. He turns to me, picks up my phone, and holds it up.

"Nina texted you."

Shit. He must have read what I texted her, and I have no idea what she texted back. My phone is so old it doesn't have a lock screen so he'd be able to just get into it by clicking on the message.

He walks toward me and looks me over.

"Don't ask her about me, understand?"

"Why?"

"Because I'm not good, Kat. And I'm definitely not good for you. Stay away from the club. Stay pure."

"I don't understand."

"You won't see me again."

With that, he turns and walks out, leaving me stunned as I drop on the edge of my bed.

6

LEV

"This is so fucking boring," Andrei complains for the tenth time this hour. "I don't see the point of sitting here like a couple of goddamned morons all day waiting for this asshole to screw us over like we know he will."

I release a breath and stare out the window, attempting to harness what little patience I have left. Being locked in a room with Andrei for twelve hours a day isn't my idea of a good time either, but this is what Vasily wants. And being that Vasily is delusional enough to believe Andrei will someday take over the business for him, it wouldn't do much good for me to shove my fist through his skull. For now, I am doomed to spend my days keeping this fuckwit in line. Vasily knows what a fuckup his son is, but he doesn't want to accept it. It's much easier for him to put me in charge of babysitting and allow Andrei to feel like he's actually doing something meaningful.

"I say we just go blow all of their fucking heads off and be done with it," he grunts, staring at the von Brandt house with a sickening smile on his face.

"That wouldn't be obvious at all." I roll my eyes. "What a genius idea, Andrei. The feds won't have any idea what happened."

"Fuck the feds," he snorts. "I have better shit to do than worry about this asshole and his family. Besides, how long are the neighbors going to be on vacation anyway?"

On that, I'm not entirely certain. The neighbor's house we're currently camped out in won't stay vacant forever, but according to the family's social media posts, it looks like they are still enjoying their time in Hawaii. It's a temporary solution to a potentially long-running problem.

"Here." I shove the binoculars in his direction. "Your turn. I need a break."

He takes the binoculars and whistles when he sees that Nina is outside in her bikini again, making the best of her parents' hot tub. "Someday, I'm going to tap that ass," he says. "Preferably before she's dead."

"You're a sick fuck, you know that?" I crack my neck and remove the phone from my pocket, opting to resume my research from earlier. Work has been getting in the way of what I really want to do, which I don't want to analyze too closely.

"What else am I supposed to do?" Andrei asks. "You sit there on your fucking phone all day looking up shit you won't even tell me about."

"That's because it's none of your concern."

He removes a small plastic canister from his shirt pocket and dumps some of the white powder onto the window ledge, snorting a line. It irritates the fuck out of me, and I'm half tempted to shove his face right through the glass, but such an act would swiftly mark my own death.

"You better go make a sandwich or find something else to do for a few minutes." Andrei unzips his pants as he resumes his visual feast of Nina von Brandt. "Shit's about to get wild in here."

Fucking disgusting. I gladly take my leave of the room and make a mental note to bring back some bleach when I return. Downstairs, I find a comfortable spot on the sofa and enjoy the rare silence while I unlock my phone.

I have another text from Alexei, but it isn't what I want to hear. Alexei is a second cousin who lives in Massachusetts, but he's become a reliable source of information when I need it. The man the Vory often refer to as the Ghost can typically find anything on anyone, given enough time. But it appears that the mystery surrounding Katerina eludes even him.

Even though he's sent me everything he has already, I opt to video call him while I have a few moments alone, hoping perhaps there is something else he can try. Alexei is mostly deaf, but he can read lips, and this is the only way to communicate with him besides text.

He answers on the third ring, and it appears I've caught him on his way out. He's just sliding into the driver's seat of his car, and his wife Talia is beside him, poking her head into the view of the screen and waving.

"Hello, Lev." She greets me with a smile.

"Talia." I give her a respectful nod. "How are you?"

"We are well," she says. "I hope you are too?"

"Always," I lie.

She seems to recognize the undercurrent of tension in my voice. "I don't want to monopolize your phone call, but you should come for a visit sometime. You've been promising you would for over a year, you know. You're welcome in our home anytime."

"Thank you," I tell her. "I appreciate that."

"Lev." Alexei angles the phone back toward himself.

"I received the files you sent me," I tell him.

"Yes, I am sorry." He shrugs. "I have not found a way to get around the three missing years of information on her record."

"Why would those records be sealed?" I ask.

"It is difficult to say." He frowns. "Typically, it's done to protect the information of a minor. But something would have had to occur. Something that the court felt it best to hide. I also suspect that since Kat changed her last name from March to Blake, she has something to hide."

His words don't put me at ease. For days, I've been trying to put Kat out of my mind, but she continues to haunt me. "What else can we do? Surely, someone can access them."

"If I knew where to look, I would have better luck," Alexei notes. "Perhaps the name of a foster parent, an institution, things of that nature. Right now, I'm just shooting blindly with the little information you were able to provide. If you get me more, I might be able to dig up something else."

Easier said than done, considering I told Katerina she would never see me again. It's not likely she will answer any questions openly now. The only alternative is Nina, and I foresee that being a problem, given the current circumstances. Nina might be a spoiled princess, but even she seems to have some morals. I don't see her ratting out her friend so easily.

"Thank you, Lyoshenka. I will see what else I can find."

"Who is this girl to you?" he asks with an arched brow. "Is she in danger?"

I know he means to ask if she is in danger from me. The question wouldn't be so offensive if it were anyone else, but I can't divulge my warring feelings for Katerina. Alexei has always been a protector of women, and for that, I can only respect him.

"She is in no danger from me," I reply. "I simply found myself curious. Her past is a mystery, and it seems like perhaps she was in danger from someone else. I only wanted to make sure she was safe."

Alexei seems to buy my half-truth for now.

"Get me more information on her, and I'll see what I can do," he says.

"Thank you." I nod. "I will let you get back to your wife and son."

"Bye, Lev!" Talia shouts from the passenger seat. "Take care."

I bid them both goodbye and disconnect the call without any sense of relief. This is proving to be more difficult than I anticipated, but as I glance at the few bits of information Alexei was able to source, I find that I can't let it go.

From what I've gathered so far, I've learned that Katerina's mother was killed when she was three. There is some mystery regarding her death, but foul play was never confirmed. From that point on, she was placed into the foster care system, jumping around from house to house. There were only brief notes in her files up until the age of fifteen, when abruptly, everything else was wiped clean.

I can't shake the feeling that something horrible happened to her. Whatever those scars are, they were no accident. I can't rewrite her history, but I tell myself that I need to ensure she's safe before I truly let her go. It's the only way I can move forward and leave her behind.

Andrei slams the door upstairs, interrupting my thoughts and reminding me there is still work to be done. He seems to have difficulty with the concept of staying quiet, and I'm tempted to slip enough Valium into his drink to knock out a horse. At least it would make my night easier.

I return upstairs with some sanitizing wipes from the kitchen and wipe down every surface near the window he may have touched before I retrieve the binoculars. Nina von Brandt has returned to the sanctuary of her home, and there is nothing of importance happening at the residence when Andrei finally exits the bathroom.

The next five hours pass with much of the same. Andrei continues to grumble about every minor inconvenience, and I focus on the von Brandt home while considering my options. A small part of me had hoped I might see Kat come to visit her friend while I was here. But a part of me is also relieved she hasn't. I don't need her getting caught up in this scandal, and I definitely don't need Andrei seeing her again.

By the time night falls, Andrei is wound tighter than a jack-in-the-box, and I'm ready to get the fuck out of here. But first, there is something else I need to do.

"Looks like they've all turned in," I tell him. "You can head back to the club."

"What about you?" he asks.

"I'll catch up with you later. I have a phone call to make."

Andrei arches his brow in question, as if I have to explain what I do on my own time to him. "You still hooking up with that drunk chick from the club?"

"No," I bite out, and his smile only grows.

"No shame in that game. She was a hot piece of ass."

Before I can grasp onto logical thought, I'm at his throat, squeezing my fingers around his thick neck.

"What the fuck, man?" he sputters and shoves me off him. "What's your fucking problem?"

"You are my goddamn problem," I snarl. "Why don't you try using your fucking brain for once before you spew every thought that comes to your mind?"

"I think you forget who you're talking to." He

brushes out the wrinkles in his shirt and snarls in my direction.

"How could I forget?" I narrow my eyes at him. "You never let anyone forget that you are Vasily's fuckup of a son who can't keep his dick in his pants or the snow out of his nose."

"Fuck you," he spits, practically foaming at the mouth. "Maybe next time I see that pretty little piece at the club, I will take her for a ride myself."

"You even try it, and you won't live to see the next day," I tell him. "Vasily's son or not."

He considers my words and then laughs like it's all a joke. I think he's fried every fucking brain cell he had left.

"Fuck this place. It's making us both crazy," he says. "I'm going to go get my dick sucked."

I glare at his retreating form and wait until the GPS tracker I have attached to his car actually disappears down the street. It will be a miracle if I survive the week without murdering him, but for now, I have other things to worry about.

When the coast is clear, I head downstairs and bail over the back fence into the von Brandt's yard. The lights in the house are off, and I know from watching them that William and his wife tend to go to sleep at the same time every night. Nina is a different matter. She could still be up, which might be a problem if she sees me before I can get to her. But either way, I'm about to find out.

It takes me all of five minutes to pick the lock on the patio door. William von Brandt is too cheap to install a security system, another sign that the guy is not as intelligent as I'd hoped. The layout of the house is almost identical to the house next door, so it isn't difficult to navigate in the dark. I take my time on the stairs, trying to remain noiseless as I traverse my way to the upper bedrooms.

The master bed is at the end of the hall, which is where William sleeps peacefully, blissfully unaware that I could smother him with a pillow right now if I really felt like it. That's just how easy it would be, yet he thinks he's untouchable, ratting us out to the feds.

Nina's door is on the opposite side of the house, and when I stand outside of it, I can't hear anything to indicate she might be awake. Vasily will want a report from me within the hour, so I don't have time to fuck around. It's now or never.

I wrap my fingers around the doorknob and turn, relieved to find that she's in her bed. But she isn't asleep. She has her back turned to the door and her headphones in as she bobs her head and taps out messages on her phone. Briefly, I consider that she might be texting Kat, and I wonder what else she had to say about me.

I tug the pistol from the back of my jeans and creep around her bed, waiting for the moment to strike. Before I can get as close as I wanted, she notices my shadow, and she peers up at me in horror. She opens her mouth to scream, and I lunge at her, slapping my palm over her lips and locking her into my grasp.

"Don't make a fucking noise," I warn her.

Her chest heaves as she tries to drag in a breath, and she nods in understanding. Nina knows what sort of business ventures her father's involved in. I doubt this is even the first time someone has threatened her this way.

"I'm going to remove my hand from your mouth," I tell her. "But understand this. If you even attempt to scream, I will put a fucking bullet in your head so fast you won't have time to think twice about it. And then I will walk down the hall and do the same to your parents. Got it?"

"Mm-hmm." She nods against my palm.

I release her and allow her a second to catch her breath before I dive into my reason for being here.

"I need some information, Nina. And you happen to be in the unfortunate position of being the only person who can help me with this task right now."

"Information about what?" Her brows pinch together in concern.

"Your friend Kat."

Her eyes narrow, and she shakes her head. "I'm not telling you anything about Kat—"

"Let's dispose of the precious sentimentalities." I tap my pistol against her cheek. "This isn't optional, in case I didn't make that clear. So, you either give me the information, or I walk down the hall and finish what I started with your father."

Her eyes widen in understanding as she begins to piece it together. "You were the one who beat him up?"

"That was merely a warning," I answer. "There won't be another one."

"You're a fucking asshole!" she snaps. "What the hell is wrong with you?"

"A lot." I shrug. "Now tell me about Kat."

She chews on her lip as she seems to consider her options, but it doesn't take her long to realize she has none. Nina knows me to be a man of my word. She doesn't doubt that I will murder her family without a second thought if she doesn't give me what I want. Her loyalties might be torn, but at the end of the day, blood always wins.

"Why don't you just ask her yourself?" she demands.

"Because I don't want to. Now what did you tell her about me?"

"I told her you were dangerous," she admits. "I warned her to stay away from you."

"Cute," I murmur. "And what else?"

"That's it," she swears.

"What were the names of her last foster parents?" I ask.

She frowns. "I don't know."

I consider her for a moment and then stand. "You can thank yourself for this."

"Wait!" She reaches out in a frantic plea. "Okay, please don't hurt my parents. I'll tell you what you want to know. At least, what I know. But just promise me you won't hurt her?"

"I'm not going to hurt her," I reply.

Nina doesn't look so sure, but she knows she's out of options. "Her last foster parents were the George family. Marie and Robert. She lived with them until she was fifteen."

"And then what?"

Nina swallows and hesitates, but one look at my face motivates her to continue. "Then she went to juvie. There was an incident with her foster dad, Robert. He was an abusive asshole, and some shit went down. She never told me exactly what."

A low simmering rage stirs in my gut as I digest her words. Katerina was locked up? When I remember the fear in her eyes the last time I saw her, it makes sense. She was afraid, ready to strike out at any moment to protect herself. This isn't something that happens overnight. Kat has been afraid her whole life, and I'm only beginning to understand why.

"The scars are from him?" My voice is rough, and Nina doesn't miss it. Her eyes soften just a fraction before she nods.

"I don't know what he did to her. I just know it was bad."

"What detention center did they send her to?"

"I have no idea." She shrugs.

"Who else was involved in the case?" I demand. "I need names. A lawyer, a judge, anything she may have mentioned."

"I don't know!" she snaps. "I swear. She doesn't like to talk about it. It's taken me years to get that much out of her."

On that, I can believe her. Katerina is not an open book. She is a locked vault with more secrets than I ever could have anticipated. But inside, I can only imagine her as a young girl with no hope and no options. Nobody to save her. She was forced to save herself, and then she was punished for it.

I close my eyes, and it physically hurts to breathe as I contemplate the things that have happened to her. If I was a decent man, I would try to help her. Fix things for her. But I know that in all likelihood, I could only ever make them worse. I failed to protect someone else once, and I vowed I would never allow that to happen again. The only way to ensure Kat's safety is to stay far away from her. But it still doesn't feel right.

"Is she safe?" I ask Nina. "There's nobody else from her past who might harm her?"

She shakes her head. "No. They are all gone now. Mrs. George moved, last I heard, and Joshua is dead."

"Joshua?" I repeat, recalling the name from Kat's dream. "Who was he?"

"Another foster kid. I don't really know the whole story with that either. Kat started to tell me once, and then she just shut down. But whatever happened, she blames herself for his death."

A door creaks open down the hall, startling both of us before there's a soft knock on Nina's door.

"You okay, honey?" her mother asks from outside. "Are you still on the phone at this hour?"

I dig the gun into her ribs and gesture for her to answer.

"I'm okay, Mom," she chokes out. "Just getting ready for bed."

"Okay," her mother replies. "Get some sleep."

The footsteps retreat, and I glance at the bedside clock. Christ, I have to get back to the club. Vasily will be expecting a report.

"Do not tell anyone we have spoken." I pull away from Nina. "And that means Kat too. Do you understand?"

"Yes." She nods forcefully. "I got it, okay. Nobody will know. Just please don't come back here."

"I won't if I can help it," I answer ominously. But the truth is, what happens next depends entirely on her father.

7

KAT

I'm not good, Kat. And I'm definitely not good for you.

After Lev leaves, I spend ten minutes just sitting there staring at the closed door, trying to wrap my brain around what just happened.

I'm not sure if I still smell that little bit of aftershave or if it's my imagination. Or just straight-up desperation.

I bend down to pick up my phone which at some point dropped to the floor.

You won't see me again.

I guess he got what he wanted, plus a bonus fuck this morning. Now he's gone, and I don't even know why I'm surprised. Or why I expected him to be different.

He only took care of me at the club because if

anything happened to me due to a bad drug, the club would be in trouble. Me kissing him like I had and practically climbing into his lap when I was high? Well, let's be honest here, that's the reason he returned the scarf. He didn't want to take advantage of me while I wasn't quite in control of myself. Not because he's such a gentleman but rather because he had to protect himself.

When he told me to stay away from the club at dinner, I don't know, maybe he didn't want to see me get hurt or into any trouble. Or maybe, again, he was protecting himself. I mean, I did use a fake ID to get in there. And it's not like it took much convincing for him to sleep with me last night.

"Ugh." I get to my feet. "I'm such a slut."

No. Fuck that. If it weren't for the very caring, upstanding, and all-around nice guy Mr. Robert George—perverted asshole—I'd still be a virgin. You can't be a slut and a virgin, right? It's just I've never been so drawn to someone like I am to Lev.

Was.

Like I *was* to Lev.

He won't be back, and I'd better get used to it.

I bite my lip to stop the tears that burn my eyes from falling. I liked him. That's all there is to it. Even if it's stupid, I did. And it hurts to know I won't see him again.

My phone buzzes with a text. Looking down at it,

I remember I never got to read Nina's message, but the text on the screen is from Sandy, a woman I work with. Her daughter's sick, and she's asking if I can come in an hour early and cover the end of her shift.

I text her back to tell her that's fine. I don't have much else going on, and I could use both the distraction and the cash.

I quickly scroll through to Nina's name to read her texts, but all I see is the deleted message notice. Two of them. I check the time. She'll be at school by now. She attends Penn State during the day like a normal nineteen-year-old. Me, I'm at the local community college for two classes this semester that I squeeze in around my work schedule.

I need to see her, but it won't be tonight, so I change into a clean uniform, grab a bag of laundry, and head to the basement to drop it into the washing machine. On my way to the diner, I text Rachel to please put my things in the dryer when she gets home and that I'll see her after class tonight. And I mostly try not to think about Lev or what happened last night or this morning.

WITH CONFLICTING SCHEDULES, it's a few days before I can see Nina. The first morning that I can, I text her.

Me: Hey. You around?

Nina: Yeah, just working on a project.

Me: Can I come over?

Nina: My dad's home, and he's got someone over but just come in around back. I'll be upstairs.

Me: I'll bring coffee.

I quickly brush my hair and twist it into a bun, grab a jacket and my purse, and head out. I don't own a car, but there's a bus stop a block away. Even though she lives in a much nicer part of town than I do, Nina's house is only about a twenty-minute ride away. There's almost a line you can draw between the middle class and the outright poor here, and as the bus drives out of my neighborhood and into hers, it's like night and day.

I get off a stop early to drop in at WaWa and pick up two large French vanilla coffees. I know it's probably fake stuff, but it's so good and way cheaper than Starbucks across the street.

It's a warm fall day, and I unzip my jacket as I walk along the quiet streets to the von Brandt home. There isn't a car parked outside, so I wonder if whoever her dad has over is gone, but I slip around the back of the house anyway.

I climb the two steps up to the porch and let myself in. The door's unlocked. Nina's mom is usually at work by now, and I'm not really sure what her dad does. He doesn't seem to have a regular schedule.

The house is quiet, so I wonder if it's just Nina and me as I make my way upstairs. Her door is cracked open, and I hear the buzz of music when I push it open all the way and see her at her desk puzzling over something on her laptop.

"Hey," I say, closing the door with the heel of my shoe.

"Hey." She peels the headphones off her head, and the music grows louder for a moment until she switches it off. She stands up, looks me over and comes to me, giving me a big hug. If I didn't know better, I'd say she's worried.

"You okay?" I ask her as she steps back and takes one of the cups of coffee.

She nods, looking me over again. "Are you?"

I drop my purse, peel off my jacket, and sit on her bed to take a sip of coffee while I think about how to answer her question.

"I don't know," I finally say.

She comes to sit beside me on the bed. "I'm sorry about the Ecstasy. I didn't know it was bad."

"You couldn't know, and you've already apologized like a hundred times. Besides, I'm fine."

"You saw Lev again, didn't you?"

"How do you know him? Who is he exactly?" I ask.

She looks away, sips her coffee. "My dad. They sorta work together sometimes," she finally says. "Why did you see him again, Kat?"

"I'd forgotten my scarf at the club, and he brought it over."

"Well, I guess that was nice of him," she says sarcastically.

"Isn't he nice?" I probe.

"I shouldn't have taken you to Delirium. We should have gone somewhere else."

"Why?"

She shakes her head. "Nothing. Just tell me what you guys did."

"He took me to dinner and told me to stay away from the club, and then we went back to his house, and…I spent the night."

"You what?"

I decide not to mention the fact we weren't super careful about it either. Although I'd just finished my period so at least I won't get pregnant.

I set my cup down on the nightstand and scrub my face with both hands. "It was great. The night, I mean. He was amazing. Nice and caring—"

She snorts.

"But then in the morning, he got weird, and I don't know. It was just…strange."

She bites her lip as if she's considering something. "Listen Kat, you gotta stay away from him. He's not a nice guy, okay?"

"Tell me who he is."

"Just trust me."

"He told me I wouldn't see him again anyway, so I guess he'll make sure I stay away."

"He told you that?"

I nod.

She nods too, and I get the feeling she wants to say something, but she doesn't, so I continue.

"It was really odd, Nina. Like night and day. He was outright icy in the morning, then he got a call which seemed to piss him off more, and I kinda jumped out of the car when we got caught in traffic."

"You jumped out of his car?" Her eyebrows disappear into her hairline.

"Well, yes. It just seemed like he really didn't want me there anyway, but then he caught up with me, and that was when things got...really weird."

"Really weird how?"

"Dark."

"What do you mean?"

"He brought me home, and then we...you know. Again."

She does that thing with her eyebrows again. "Christ, Kat! Of all the people you could pick!"

"But it was different. He was...different."

"Different how?"

"Not as caring, I guess." I pause, and she doesn't seem surprised. "Who is he? I wish someone would tell me. He deleted the texts you sent me, so I didn't even get to read them."

"Well that explains things."

"Explains what things?"

She gets up, walking to the window. "Nothing. Shit."

I go over to her and look outside to find a man in a dark suit walk out of her house and down the street.

"Who's that?"

"I don't know. I just hope my dad isn't being stupid."

"What's going on, Nina?"

Her phone dings, and she turns to pick it up off her desk. "Look, I'm late."

"You know about him. You know who he is. You knew at the club, and he scared you."

Her face goes a little paler. "His uncle is into some bad shit. That's all."

"He works for his uncle."

"Yeah, well, do the math and stay away from him. He's bad news." She sighs. "I really gotta go. I'll walk you out."

"At least tell me what kind of bad shit."

She stops and looks at me with an expression of worry and pity and pretty much nothing good.

"Russian mafia, Kat. The fucking Russian mafia kind."

SIX WEEKS LATER

8

KAT

True to his word, Lev pretty much disappears from my life. There are moments when I feel the hair on the back of my neck stand on end, and every time that happens, hope bubbles up in my belly.

But that hope is quickly followed by a not-so-little pang of disappointment when I turn around and realize it's not him. Realize he meant it when he said I wouldn't see him again. It doesn't stop me from thinking about him, though. That hasn't changed. Well, maybe it's gotten worse, but I'm hoping my trip to the drug store on my way home from work will put my mind at ease.

Rachel is unpacking groceries when I walk in a little after nine at night. She's working a late shift tonight.

"Hey," she says when she sees me.

I set my bag down to help her unpack. We split the grocery shopping, so we each go once a week, and then we split the cost down the middle, which works really well.

"How was work?" she asks.

"Long. But I got decent tips tonight."

I open one of the plastic bags, and my stomach turns when I smell fish.

"Salmon was on sale. I got two pieces," Rachel says with a proud smile. "You liked it last time."

I did. I do. But tonight, I'm going to be sick. "I just ate at the diner," I lie. "Maybe we can freeze it?"

"Sure." We unpack the groceries, and I'm holding my breath almost the entire time. As soon as everything's put away, I pick up my things and go into the bathroom. I lock the door that leads to Rachel's bedroom and take out my purchase. I count the days again, although I've already counted a dozen times.

Lev and I had sex four times. We used a condom two of those times. I'd just finished my period three days before, so there's really no way. I mean, there's really, really no way I can be pregnant. It would be insanely unlucky.

Although hasn't that always been the sort of luck I attract?

I've gone back and forth with this logic for days now, and there's no denying the fact that I'm late.

I take the pregnancy test out of its package and set it down on the toilet to pee on the stick. I know how this goes. It's not the first time I've done this. But it's been four years since I've had a scare.

The results show up pretty quickly. I know it says to wait, but I know it's almost immediate. And like I knew it would, that little pink plus sign shows up right away.

My heart sinks into my belly. I drop the stick in the sink and grab the second test and pee on that, too. There's a third one in the box too, but I don't bother. I have my answer. Had it before these little plus signs.

I'm pregnant.

A knock on the door startles me. "Kat, you okay in there?" Rachel asks.

Crap. "Yeah. Sorry, I know you need to shower before work. I'll be out in a sec."

Cleaning up, I pick up the tests and drop them back into their box and then put the box back into the plastic bag. I wash my hands and walk back into my bedroom to process.

I'm pregnant.

I'm pregnant with Lev's baby.

"Shit."

My hands shake as I pick up my phone, and with

fingers shaking so badly, it takes three attempts to get my text to Nina to make sense.

Me: I need to see you.

No answer even though she's online.

I start to type another message but decide to call her instead. The call goes right to voicemail. "Nina. Fuck." A sob escapes. "I really need to see you. I'm on my way."

Pulling on my pink scarf and jacket, I rush out of the apartment and run to the bus stop. It's raining again. Sheets of it drenching me, but I barely notice. A woman I run into here almost daily says hello, but I can't manage my usual smile. At least the bus is on time tonight, and I'm grateful for the burst of heat when I get inside.

Pregnant.

I'm pregnant.

I walk down the aisle, catching myself on the back of a chair when the bus lurches forward. My gaze slides to the seats reserved for the elderly and pregnant women.

I'm fucking pregnant.

"Fuck."

I sit down at the back of the bus and stare absently out the window. I'm in a daze for the entire ride, and only when I'm getting off the bus does my phone vibrate in my back pocket.

I reach back to grab it.

Nina: Not a good time. Parents are having the mother of all fights.

Me: I'm already here. A block away. I really need to talk to you.

It's darker than usual on Nina's street. The lamps seem to be broken out, but maybe it's just the rain. A dark van is parked a few houses away. I notice it because it's so out of place with its blacked-out windows.

I'm about to walk up to the front door when I hear Nina's mom and dad. They're arguing. And it's loud. Even with the windows closed, I can hear them.

"Kat," Nina calls out from her upstairs window. Her room is dark, which is strange. I guess she was waiting for me. "Come around back."

I nod and slip around, my Chucks getting stuck in the muddy lawn. The fighting grows louder when I open the back door, and I hear Nina's mom asking her dad how he could be so stupid.

I take my muddy shoes off and leave them at the back door. Making as little noise as possible, I creep up the stairs to find Nina waiting with her door open. Her parents fight a lot, and she usually takes it in stride, but tonight, something's different.

"Hey," I say.

She puts her finger to her lips and pulls me into her room. She closes and locks the door.

When I go to flip the light switch, she stops me.

"You okay?" I ask her, suddenly worried about her. I slip off my scarf and set my purse down but don't take my jacket off.

"You can't be here, Kat."

"What's going on?"

Her face is pale, and she looks like she might throw up. She gets up and opens her desk drawer, but instead of looking inside it, she bends down to slide her hand underneath it, and when she turns to me, I see she's holding a flash drive.

"What's that?"

"I stole it from my dad's study. It's what they're fighting about."

"What is it?"

"Fuck, Kat. I'm going to be sick." She hands the drive to me and rushes into her bathroom. I hear her retch, and the sound makes me nauseous, but I go in after her to at least hold her hair back.

"What's going on, Nina?"

"My dad did something really stupid. So freaking stupid." She's crying, wiping the back of her hand across her mouth.

I wet a washcloth and hand it to her.

"What did he do?"

"Stole something."

I look down at what I'm holding then back at her.

"You need to get out of here. They're coming. If they don't find it, maybe they'll believe him when he tells them he doesn't have it. I doubt it. They'll beat the shit out of him but—"

"Who? Who's coming?"

We both hear a vehicle then, and she runs ahead of me to her bedroom window. "Shit!" She turns to me before I make it to see outside. "You need to go. Now!"

"What—"

"Fuck. Where are your shoes, Kat?"

"They were muddy. I left them—"

"Never mind. Take mine. I'll call you tomorrow. Don't come back until I call you, okay?" She shoves my purse at me and takes off her boots as I hear voices downstairs.

Voices I recognize?

"Is that...?"

Nina stares at me. "Please go. Get that thing out of here." I barely have time to pull on her boots as she shoves me toward the window along the side of the house. This is the one she uses to sneak into when she's late. I've climbed the trellis with her, so I wrap my purse across my shoulder as I swing a leg out.

"Come with me!" I tell her.

"I can't. They'll come after me if I go. They know I'm here. Go!"

I climb out, the rain and my own anxiety making the trellis sweaty. Nina closes the window and turns away just as a light goes on in her room, and I duck out of sight. Climbing down fast, I lose my footing once and just barely catch myself. I only make it to the ground as I hear a quick, sharp pop, and although I've never heard a gun fired anywhere but on TV before, I know that's what that sound is. I know it.

I back away from the house when I hear another one of those pops. Tears stream down my face as I turn to the street, thinking to run to the bus stop because where else would I go?

But then I see the Audi. It's parked at the far end of the road, and I only see it because of another car's headlights passing on the cross street.

And I'm grateful for not having been able to eat today. For having vomited everything I did eat back up because I feel sick. I feel sick as I run through the backyard and into the shadow of the woods that separate this property from the next.

I feel sick as I hear one more pop, and I know Nina won't be calling me tomorrow. I know it like I knew Joshua wouldn't make it out of the basement that last night. That he'd never see the light of day again.

I drop to my hands and knees then, dry heaving. I reach for my scarf, the one Joshua gave me, but it's not there. I took it off on Nina's bed, and in our rush, I forgot it.

I do the math again.

Lev works for the Russian mafia. I look down at the drive I'm still gripping and do some more math.

Nina's dad probably stole this from them.

Shit.

Lev will recognize my scarf. And whether or not he knows I have the thumb drive, he'll know I was at the house. He'll realize I know he was there. And that I know what he did.

And he'll come to return that scarf again. But this time, he won't be inviting me to dinner. He'll be putting a bullet in my head.

9

LEV

The pulse in my neck throbs as I shift the car into park and glance up the street. Andrei is already here, and he's not in his car, which means he's either already in the house or close to it. *Shit.*

He's coked out and amped up, and I have no idea how this is going to go down. Vasily gave us very specific orders, but whether Andrei is capable of following them is another question.

I stuff my pistol into the back of my jeans and check the street before darting toward the house. Sure enough, when I creep around the back, the door is already split wide open.

I step inside, nearly tripping over a few scattered shoes. The place is eerily quiet, and I'm on high alert as I venture farther into the house. Fucking Andrei can't wait two goddamn minutes. Now I have no idea what the hell I'm walking into.

When I turn the corner to the staircase, something cracks me in the back of the head, sending white-hot pain through my skull. *Mother fuck.*

I double over and blink a few times before William von Brandt tackles me to the floor from behind. I don't even know where he came from. But from the shattered pottery around us, it's apparent he tried to take me out with a fucking vase.

I elbow him in the gut and manage to knock the wind out of him long enough to regain my balance. Blood drips down my temple as I land three solid punches to his face and roll over on top of him. A scream reverberates off the walls upstairs, and William freezes. So do I. Motherfucking Andrei. *What the hell is he doing?*

"Andrei!" I yell for him, but he doesn't answer.

This wasn't the plan. All we had to do was come in here and take care of William. We were supposed to wait until they were asleep. It should have been a quick job. But as usual, Andrei is off his goddamn head, and shit's going sideways really quick.

"Please," William begs as I jam the pistol into his throat. "Don't hurt them. They have nothing to do with this."

"Where is the drive?" I bite out.

"I don't have it." He shakes his head. "I swear to you."

"Don't fucking lie to me." I slam his head into the floor as another scream echoes upstairs. This time, a gunshot swiftly follows it.

Son of a bitch.

William resumes his fight, struggling to free himself. He attempts to wrestle the gun from my hand as I clock him in the face three more times. I need to get upstairs, but I can't just leave him here.

"Tell me where the goddamn drive is!" I wrap my palm around his throat and squeeze as I jam the pistol into his rib cage.

"I don't have it!" he spits. "I'm telling you the truth. It's gone. Please, my wife—"

I squeeze the trigger and blood explodes across my face. William's chest begins to rattle, and blood gurgles between his lips as he shakes his head, still pleading with me even as he's minutes away from death.

"You did this," I snarl. "You made this bed for yourself. Talking to the goddamn feds? Stealing from Vasily? What the fuck did you think would happen?"

Another gunshot sounds upstairs, and this time, a sick feeling washes over me as my adrenaline starts to slow. Leaving William on the floor, I climb the stairs two at a time, pausing on the landing, where Elizabeth von Brandt is lying with a bullet wound to the head. Her eyes are wide open, and she's far past saving. From Nina's room, I can hear Andrei cursing under his breath.

Stepping over the dead body, I move down the hall and wipe the blood from my eyes before pushing open the door. But I'm already too late. Nina is lying in pool of her own blood, her pants torn off and her face beaten to a bloody pulp. She's dead. *Kat's best friend is dead.*

"What the fuck have you done?" I charge at Andrei and tackle him to the floor, slamming my fist into his face until the bones in my fingers splinter and his blood covers my knuckles.

When I finally manage to pull myself away, my chest heaves with the reality I can't shake. He fucking killed them. He killed them both.

"The bitch bit me," he groans, rolling around on the floor in pain.

"That's the least of what you deserve." I spit at him. "You fucking worthless sack of shit. Who told you to touch her? Who told you to kill them?"

He doesn't answer. And when he stumbles to his feet, I consider throwing him out the goddamn window. How much would Vasily really miss him? How hard would it be to convince him that this waste of human space fucked everything up and William shot him? But even as I consider it, I know it's only a fantasy. The unspoken agreement is that I need to keep Andrei alive and out of trouble. The minute he's no longer breathing, I might as well sign my death warrant too.

"Go downstairs and check on William. Make sure he's dead," I tell him. "I can't stand to look at you right now."

"We need to find the drive," he answers sheepishly.

"Don't you think I know that?" I shake my head. "I'm going to clean up your fucking mess here, and while I do that, you can look downstairs. Do you think you can manage that?"

"Yes," he grunts. "I got it."

He disappears out the door, and my eyes drift to Nina. The urge to retch overtakes me, but I choke it back down as I consider what I have to do. I can't think of her as Kat's friend anymore. I can't think of this in any way other than what it is now. Damage control.

But I also can't leave her here like this. Disgraced and humiliated. Carefully, I dig through her dresser drawers and find a pair of pajama pants. It might not make much of a difference, considering what I'll have to do now, but this is the last thing I can do for her.

I dress her and lay her back in her bed, covering her up. And for a full minute, I just stand there, wondering when this became my life. My chest is heavy when I drape the blanket over Nina's face, but there isn't time to consider how fucked up this situation is. At the end of the day, all I know how to do is get on with the job of surviving. Cleaning up Andrei's messes and doing Vasily's bidding. A burden I resent more and more with each passing day.

As I dissect the room, tearing through every possible hidey-hole for the drive, I fantasize about a different life. A life where I have the answers that brought me into this world in the first place. A life where my mother's death hasn't gone unavenged, and I can actually look myself in the mirror at night. But these are just empty thoughts, built upon a crumbling foundation. I've been working for my uncle for ten years now, and I am still no closer to having the answers I seek. The hope of leaving this existence behind abandoned me long ago, but I'm still here, still functioning on autopilot. And right now, I'm not any closer to finding the drive that Vasily sent us here for in the first place. The drive that William von Brandt knew very well could sink us.

Just when I think I've turned over every inch of Nina's room, something catches my eye. The familiar shade of pink from a scarf I know all too well. Ice coats my veins as I grab the ratty old scarf and bring it to my nose, inhaling.

Katerina.

She was here. But when? A glance at the window only intensifies the churning in my gut. It's not fully closed, and just outside, a few strands of faded Magenta hair stick to the trellis. She left in a hurry.

Fuck.

My heart slams into my rib cage as I consider what might have happened if she hadn't. But what's worse is the fact she may have seen something or heard something. What did Nina tell her? Has she already called the cops?

My brain is firing off questions faster than I can answer them, but the only thing I know for certain is that I need to get the fuck out of here and find her, fast.

"Andrei!" I yell down the stairs. "We need to go. Have you found anything?"

"No," he grunts.

"I have one more room to clear," I tell him. "Start looking for some accelerant. Anything you can find."

He mumbles something I can't understand as I tear through the von Brandt's master suite. But my search turns up nothing. There are only two possibilities left. Either the drive is no longer here, or it will go down in flames with the rest of the evidence. There isn't time for anything else.

"This ought to do it." Andrei appears with two gas cans he must have found in the garage.

I nod and take one of them. "I'll handle the upper level. You get downstairs. Make sure to douse William, the drapes, anything that will burn."

He limps away and does as I request without protest, still nursing his wounds from earlier. Vasily will probably have something to say about me beating his face in, but I'm long past giving a fuck.

I douse the carpet, the beds, and Nina's body with gasoline. When Andrei shouts that he's done downstairs, I grab the pack of matches I found in the bathroom and set flame to the beds and the carpet. Downstairs, I repeat the process on William's body and the other places that Andrei points out. The smoke is already starting to fill the house, and when the fire alarms are triggered, I gesture for Andrei.

On our way out the door, he nearly trips over a muddy pair of shoes. The same shoes I tripped over on my way in. And it isn't until he looks at them and his brows pinch together that I realize the scarf isn't the only thing Kat left behind.

"Whose shoes are those?" he asks.

"Probably Nina's," I lie.

He shakes his head. "I've never seen her wear them. And she hasn't left the house today, so why would they be muddy?"

The one time I need Andrei to be a dumb fuck, he starts piecing shit together.

"Then they're Elizabeth's. Who gives a shit? We need to go."

"There was a scarf upstairs too." His brows pinch together. "That drunk chick from the club. She had one just like it."

"Andrei, we need to get the fuck out of here. The cops are coming," I bark.

He takes one more long look at the shoes and then bolts out the door. I should be thinking about my exit strategy, potential witnesses, and a million other problems that have just presented themselves, but there's only one thing on my mind now.

Andrei knows, and I am so fucked.

I TOLD Andrei I would meet him back at the club, and he bought it for now. When I pull up to Kat's apartment complex, I'm not entirely sure how this will play out. It's not even dinnertime yet. People are still up, getting home from work and watching TV. It's not like I can drag her out of here in broad daylight. But I can't leave her here either.

My fist rattles the door in its frame before Rachel finally pokes her head out through the chain.

"What do you want?" She glares.

"I need to see Kat."

"She isn't here," she hisses.

"Bullshit."

"Look, asshole. I don't know who you are—"

I slam my shoulder into the door without warning, and Rachel stumbles back in horror as I enter the apartment and shut the door behind me.

"Don't scream." I shake my finger at her when she opens her mouth. "I don't want to hurt you, but if you make a scene, I'll tape your fucking mouth shut."

Her eyes dart to the door. She considers her options, but it doesn't take her long to accept that she's trapped.

"Kat isn't here," she repeats. "I don't know what you want, but—"

"Where is she?" I glance down the hall toward her room.

"She bailed." Rachel glares up at me. "I don't know what's going on. She just came home, freaked out, and said she had to leave. She grabbed a bag of clothes, and she was gone. That's all I know."

Christ.

I don't want to believe it, but the empty silence in the apartment only seems to confirm Rachel's account. If Kat was here, she'd be out in the living room by now, trying to defend her friend. That much I know.

"Show me." I gesture for Rachel to move, and she hesitates.

"C'mon. I don't have all fucking day. Show me her room."

Finally, Rachel staggers down the hall, glancing over her shoulder every couple of feet to check if I'm still here. She doesn't trust me, and I can't say that I blame her.

"Satisfied?" She crosses her arms when we reach the end of the hall.

Kat's room is in complete disarray. Clothes strewn across the bed, her dresser drawers open. She was in a hurry all right, which only manages to confirm what I suspected. She saw something she shouldn't have, and now she's in the wind.

"Where did she go?" I pick up one of her sweaters from the floor and toss it onto the bed.

"I'm telling you, I don't know." Rachel shakes her head. "She wouldn't say. She was totally spooked by something, and she just kept telling me she had to go."

I pinch the bridge of my nose to temper the headache I feel coming on. "Where are your garbage bags?"

"What?" Her eyes narrow.

"Where do you keep the garbage bags?" I repeat.

"In the kitchen."

"Start folding her clothes," I order. "Don't try anything stupid."

She sits down on the bed with an exasperated

sigh and starts folding. I retrieve the garbage bags from the kitchen and return to help her. Kat doesn't have a lot, but what she does have is in this room. And if I find her, I want to make sure she has the rest of her belongings. But more importantly, I need to know that nobody else will come looking for them here.

"Do you have somewhere else to go?" I ask Rachel as we stuff two bags full of everything Kat left behind.

"What do you mean?" She blinks. "I live here."

"Not anymore." I grab a wad of cash from my wallet and toss it onto the bed beside her. "It isn't safe here for you either. You need to leave. Tonight. Do you understand?"

"What the hell is going on?" She swallows. "What did Kat get herself into?"

"She didn't do anything wrong," I answer roughly. "The only mistake she made was meeting me."

"I knew you were fucking trouble." Rachel glances around the apartment with a sentimentality I haven't felt in years. Not since I had a home with my mother.

"Look, I'm going to lay it all out for you." I tug the handles of the garbage bag shut and tie them together. "You pack your shit and leave. Find another place to live. Stay in a hotel. Do whatever you gotta do. But don't come back here. Don't call the cops. Forget you ever knew Kat, and as far as you're concerned, you never met me. If you follow those simple rules, you get to live. It really is that fucking simple."

"Who are you?" she whispers.

"I think you know who I am." I offer her a dark look. "So don't make me say it."

"Where the fuck have you been?" Vasily snarls.

"I thought I had a tail." My jaw flexes as I glance at Andrei, cowering in the corner while he nurses a whiskey. "I drove around the city for a bit to make sure everything was clear."

Vasily seems to consider my words, nodding when he's satisfied that I'm telling the truth. "What the fuck happened, Levka?"

"Ask your son." I glare at Andrei. "He can't keep his dick in his pants, and he was high as a goddamn kite. He lost his shit, and everything went sideways. There was nothing I could do."

Vasily growls and begins to pace the length of the room. "And the drive?"

"We couldn't find it."

"I don't like loose ends." He stares at me with a stony expression. "You know that."

"Then next time, send me and leave Andrei here to do what he does best."

Vasily shakes his head. "Enough. I will deal with Andrei. For now, I want you scouring the city. Check everywhere that William von Brandt ever set foot in the door. We need to find that drive."

I nod my assurances and turn to go, but he stops me. "There is something Andrei said. It concerns me."

"What is it?" I turn to meet his gaze.

"He mentioned a girl who was at the club. Someone you took home. Andrei seems convinced that she was at the von Brandt's house. She may have seen something."

Tension bleeds into my muscles, and I can only hope Vasily hasn't noticed. "I will take care of her."

"No more loose ends," he grunts. "Do you understand, Lev?"

"No loose ends," I repeat.

"I want proof when it's done. Something tangible. Don't forget where your loyalties lie."

Again, I force myself to nod.

"Nothing comes before blood, Uncle," I answer solemnly. "I give you my word."

FOUR YEARS LATER

10

KAT

Today is the anniversary.

"Mommy?"

I blink, glancing in the rearview mirror, and try to smile. "Yes, baby?"

"Your eyes are shiny." Josh scrunches up his face. "Are you sad?"

"Oh sweetheart, I'm not sad. See." I stretch that smile wide.

"You're beautiful," he says, the word coming out more like booful, which makes that smile on my face authentic.

"And so are you."

"Mommy! Boys aren't beautiful."

"No, you're right. You're handsome." I turn into the parking lot of the school and drive around the circle of moms dropping off kids for the day. It's a primary school where I work as a teacher's aide in the kindergarten class while Josh is looked after in the preschool.

There aren't many options for single moms, and I feel pretty lucky to have found the school. Josh and I rent a small cabin nearby, and the school is the only one for the three tiny towns that surround ours, so although it's not big by Philadelphia standards, it's big enough. Estes Park, which is about an hour away, is the biggest town nearest ours.

Even though the job isn't the best paying job in the world, there's no way I'd be able to afford daycare any other way, so for now, this is what works. And it's on track for what I want to eventually do, which is teach. I've already registered to start online classes to continue toward my degree next semester.

I park my Jeep in one of the empty spaces, listening to the engine do its gurgle as I switch it off. It's going to have to go to the shop soon and before winter sets in, but it's an expense I just don't want to think about now.

I turn around in my seat and look at Josh, who's "'reading.'" I pluck the book, *Good Night, Gorilla*, from his hand and give it back right side up.

"We'll have to return that to the library today."

"Okay."

"Do you know what you want to read next?"

"*Skippyjon Jones and the Big Bones*!"

"Again?"

He nods enthusiastically, his smile widening. His chocolate eyes sparkle, and he gets that dimple in his right cheek, and I falter, my heart giving a little flutter as it skips a beat. He looks so much like Lev. He didn't at first. When he was born, his eyes were a deep blue, and he didn't look like either of us, but I swear every day he's more and more like his father.

"Alright then. Ready for school, kiddo?"

"Yep."

I climb out of the front seat, zip my coat against the cold Colorado wind, and open the back door. Josh holds his arms out for me to unstrap him and lift him out. It's too hard for him to get out of the buckles of the car seat just yet.

I slip my hands under his pudgy arms. The puffy coat makes him look like the Michelin Man.

Lifting him out, I give him a little squeeze, then set him on the ground and grab his Minions backpack, which is empty but for his lunch. I unzip it, slip his book inside, close the door, and take his small hand in mine. He'll need new gloves for winter too. His little fingers are already cold.

"We'll go get some gloves after school too."

"After the library?"

"After the library," I say as we walk to the front entrance of the school.

A whisper on the wind has me turning toward the woods that border the back of the property. Dense pines make it impossible for light to penetrate, and for a moment, I think I see movement.

It's been like this for the past few weeks. I've felt it like I did before, that raising of the hairs on the back of my neck. That slight scent that I don't know if I imagine or if it just happens to be someone else wearing the same aftershave Lev wore. I don't even know how I still remember that detail and wish I could forget.

"Miss Katie!" a little girl calls out, making me jump.

I turn away from the woods.

I'm just on edge because of the anniversary. Because today is the day Nina and her family were killed. Well, tonight is. It's the night I found out I was pregnant with Lev's baby. The night I'd gone to her house for help when she slipped that flash drive into my hand and made me leave, made me promise not to come back until she called me.

She never did call.

The house burned down that night, and three charred bodies were found inside. Foul play. Arson. Bullets.

"What do you say, Katie?"

I give a shake of my head. Katie. Sometimes I forget to answer to it.

"I'm sorry?" I ask.

"Why don't you and Josh come over for dinner next week on Friday? It's Emma's half-birthday, and we're getting a cake," Emma's dad, Luke Foreman, says. He's a nice guy. In his mid-forties, he lost his wife early to cancer.

"Can we, Mommy?" Josh asks. He tugs on my hand, and I lean down. He raises his eyebrows and leans in close. "There's cake," he whispers loudly.

Luke smiles and winks at me when I straighten. "Sounds great," I say, although I need to be careful not to give Luke the wrong idea. He asked me out to dinner a while back, and I told him it was against school policy to date a parent, which wasn't a lie, but it wasn't the only reason. After everything that happened, I haven't really been interested in anyone. Just keeping myself and Josh safe is my priority because I'm not sure if Lev or the men he works with have found out that I was there that night. That I have the flash drive they were looking for. That I know they killed Nina's family.

But I'm not taking any chances. I can't because it's not just my life at stake now. I won't let anything happen to my baby and that includes losing me. Because I know what happens when you're alone in the world. I know the monsters that prey on those weaker than them, and I will not allow monsters into Josh's life.

And besides, I'm not interested in Luke as anything more than a friend. Since Lev, I haven't been interested in anyone.

Another gust of wind has me clutching Josh's hand tighter.

"They're saying it's going to be an early blizzard," Luke says.

"I hope not." The first bell rings. "We'd better get inside."

The morning passes as usual, and although I'd normally spend my lunch hour with Josh, today, I put on my coat and hat and head out to the parking lot.

They're predicting a foot of snow already, and a glance up at the darkening sky confirms it. Josh and I have lived here for a little over three years, and although I love the snow, I hate driving in it and hope it won't be as bad as they're forecasting.

Getting into the Jeep, I glance at the space in the woods that had caught my attention earlier, but nothing's there now. And it doesn't look as dark and foreboding as it had early this morning.

Pulling out of the parking lot, I head to the florist in town to pick up the bouquet. It's ready for me, and I'm grateful for that. I won't have much time before I have to get back to the school even though the lead teacher in my room knows I may be a few minutes late.

I set the flowers on the passenger's seat and drive out of town. The elegant, long white callas look out of place on the worn upholstery of the Jeep.

Light flurries have already begun to fall as I navigate the curving road up to Daniel's Point. I found the overlook by accident. It's not easy to get to, which means I don't often run into anyone out there, but today, I'm anxious as the road rises in elevation and visibility becomes an issue.

Switching on the radio for company, I listen absently to songs periodically broken by static until, twenty minutes later, I reach the turnoff for the overlook.

Tires grate on loose stones as I park the Jeep as close to the point as I can. I pull my knit cap on, pick up the flowers, and climb out, my boots crunching on those same stones. I walk around the barrier and onto the barely recognizable trail, and for a moment, the only sound is that of my boots on a random branch or dried up leaf.

There's a stillness here. Where Josh and I live is quiet too, but here, it's different than Philadelphia. It's like the mountains eat sound, and when I stop to listen to it, to hear it, it has a way of reassuring me and filling me with peace. It's the strangest thing, but when I get to the overlook, and it's like the world opens up to me, I just stand there and listen to that sound. A part of me wishes it could stay here forever and never go back.

My mom died when I was three in a car accident on a road much like this one in that it was remote and mostly deserted. We were stranded for two days before they found us. It had been fall, too. Fall is an unlucky time for me.

I shouldn't have survived that accident, but somehow, I did.

My phone buzzes in my pocket, and I'm grateful for the interruption. I dig it out and switch off the alarm I'd set for myself. I have about ten minutes before I have to head back, and I set a second alarm just in case. I walk as far as I can on the overhanging stone and crouch to lay the flowers down.

Nina loved calla lilies. They were her favorite flowers. She'd always complain that no guys ever sent her flowers.

I spend a few minutes arranging the four long stems. One for each year since she's been gone.

"I miss you," I tell the wind. "I should have made you come with me that night." I dig into my pockets for a tissue but don't find any, so I wipe my eyes with the backs of my hands. I'm going to need mittens too because my fingers are frozen.

But at that moment, I feel it again.

The back of my neck prickles, the hair stands on end, and that feeling is back. Like someone's watching.

I freeze, unable or unwilling to turn around. To see.

Something crunches behind me, a twig, and I gasp, straighten, and spin, reaching into my pocket and digging out the pocketknife. I keep one in every pocket and in every bag. I have since I left Philly.

I step backward, trip, and just catch myself as a deer springs across the path and into the dense cover of trees. I exhale a loud breath and clutch my stomach, my body relaxing in relief.

A deer. It's just a deer.

I laugh out loud, but it sounds a little crazy, and the second alarm on my phone goes off, warning me I'll be late if I don't leave. I walk quickly back to the Jeep, almost running by the time I get to it.

The remote doesn't work, and with my fingers as cold as they are, it takes several tries to get the key into the lock. When I'm finally in, I slap the locks down and start the engine. I've never been in such a hurry to get away from here. Never been so spooked, not for a long time now.

I'm safe. It was just a deer. I'm jumpy because of the anniversary. That's all.

I keep telling myself that as I drive a little too fast down the mountain road, only glancing in my rearview mirror when I think I see a flash of headlights, but in the cover of low clouds and the thickening snow, I see nothing. I'm alone on the road. Just me. And after one more turn, I'm back in civilization.

Safe.

11

LEV

Katie fucking March.

She gets out of her piece of shit Jeep and walks around to the back. For a split second, I question if it's really her. The magenta hair is gone, replaced by a natural red. Her clothes aren't the same either. She's wearing a winter coat and boots, but they look cheap and sad, and I don't like it.

I don't like any of this fucking scenario. When Alexei told me he'd finally gotten a hit on her, it was difficult to accept. Even now, I still can't be certain. Not until she turns and glances in the direction of the woods, as if she can feel me watching her.

My breath pauses, and I can't even bring myself to blink. I know it's impossible, but it feels like she's looking right at me, and now, it's undeniable. Katerina has been holed up in the mountains of Colorado, hiding from me.

Adrenaline rushes through my veins as I consider what happens now. I have searched for her so long, compounding my frustrations into a low simmering rage. She ran out on me, and she took something very important with her. Logically, I know what I have to do. What Vasily expects of me. But seeing her after so long has triggered something else in me. Something I never expected to feel again.

Katerina returns her attention to the back seat of the Jeep, and in a split second, everything changes. I don't know what I'm expecting, but when she hauls out a little boy, it sure as fuck isn't that.

My fingers turn rigid around the binoculars as she glances around one more time and heads toward the entrance. Surely, he can't be hers? Ice enters my lungs as I drag in a deep, painful breath and release it. She works at a school. Perhaps he's a student here. But logically, I know that can't be true.

I can't tell from this distance how old the boy might be. But I can only surmise that Kat didn't wait long to run off and set up a new life with somebody else. That betrayal burns the blood in my veins as I watch them with an intensity I can't shake. It only gets worse when another man approaches her. They seem familiar, but not familiar enough that he could be a husband. Regardless, it's evident that he wants to find his way into her pants as he tosses out easy smiles and pretty words.

He looks like a fucking douchebag in khakis, and I'm willing to bet he bought a pair in every color from his local Sears before they went out of business. Motherfucker.

I retrieve my phone and snap a few photos, aware they are probably too blurry to do anything with. But I send them to Alexei anyway, hoping he can give me some background on this piece of shit sniffing around Kat like he has a right to.

She disappears into the school with the little boy in tow, and I spend the day staking out her environment. It's fucking freezing up here in the mountains, but I can't bring myself to move. Now that I've found her, I'm not willing to let her out of my sight.

At lunch, she takes a short drive up into the mountains and spreads some flowers out along the overlook. Today, it has been four years since that clusterfuck of events transpired. And it's clear that Kat is still in mourning for her friend. A fact that grates the raw wound in my chest whenever I think about Nina von Brandt and her mother. They didn't deserve to die that way, and I have every reason to believe Kat thinks I'm responsible for it. Why else would she be here out in the middle of nowhere?

I follow her back to the school, careful to keep my distance, and she spends the rest of the afternoon there. When the bell rings, it isn't long before she's traipsing back out to her Jeep with the little boy in tow. When I consider that someone else touched her and impregnated her, acid coats my throat. I don't want to believe it. But the only alternative to that notion is something else that seems too farfetched for me to accept.

Regardless, I follow them home and park down the street, camping out with a decent vantage point where I can watch the small cabin she calls home. As the hours pass, I catch her glancing out the window a few times. She can feel me here, but she doesn't trust her judgment.

Eventually, around nine o'clock, the lights go out, and the house falls quiet. Nobody else comes home. And so goes the routine over the next several days as I study her, learning her patterns. I take notes of everything she does. When she shops for groceries, when she makes dinner, when she takes her break at the school. Vasily calls me for constant updates, asking where I am. I tell him I'm in Florida, and that any day now, I'll have something tangible. That proof he requested four years ago.

On the fifth day, I can't wait any longer. I break into the school and wait in the janitor's closet before she gets to work. It's a risk, but I manage to go unnoticed until lunchtime, when she leaves her classroom. In her purse, I find her keys, and I slip out of the building, taking them down to the local hardware store to make copies.

When I return to the school, I dump her set near the front entrance and watch as the khaki-wearing motherfucker comes to her rescue during the ensuing chaos. He finds the keys during her minor freak-out, and he gets to be the hero. But it doesn't end there.

I expect her to get in her Jeep and go home the same as she does every night. But tonight, she follows him back to his house. And then she goes inside. I park on the street, contemplating the various ways I might murder him. Burning his face off with a blowtorch seems like a good idea. But as I watch them through the window, eating cake and celebrating what appears to be a birthday, it occurs to me that her heart isn't in it. The smile on her face is polite but forced. And soon after the celebrations, she takes the opportunity to leave.

It doesn't relieve me as much as I'd hoped. Because even if she isn't staying tonight, that doesn't mean she never will. I shift the car into gear and drive around town for a while, trying to clear my head. Inevitably, I end up back at her place after dark. She's already asleep when I slip in, and for the first time, I can finally smell her again. I drag in lungsful of that scent like an addict, and then touch everything in her space as if to mark my territory.

Chapter 11

I don't know what the fuck is wrong with me. I just know that when I stand on the threshold of her bedroom, watching her sleep, there is finally peace in my soul. For all of two minutes, until I realize that I came here to kill her. That was the job I set out to do. A thought that was much easier when there was distance and years between us. Now everything is fucked up again, and the only thing I understand is that I can't. Not tonight.

I spend the night on her sofa, staring up at the ceiling, until I hear the creak of her floorboards when she gets up in the morning. At that point, the shower turns on, and a soft throaty hum filters out into the living room as she begins to wash herself. I know I shouldn't, but my feet are moving before my mind can conjure up all the reasons this is a bad idea.

The bathroom door is cracked open, and through the steam, I catch a glimpse of her naked form behind the glass shower wall. Fuck me. She's even more beautiful than I remembered. A little softer, a little curvier, and without a doubt, the sweetest poison I ever tasted.

I close my eyes and inhale her scent before I realize how fucking blatant I'm being. If she catches me right now, things could end badly. I need more information before I confront her. I need more time.

Slipping back into her bedroom, I find a cozy

spot beneath the bed. When she returns from the shower and drops her towel, I bite back a groan. It would be tempting to bend her over right now and reacquaint her with my cock, but that isn't on the menu today.

It takes her another forty minutes to get her and the boy she calls Josh ready and out the door. A name I remember well, and one I have every intention of uncovering the mystery behind. But first, I take a tour of her bedroom, searching through the drawers and closet. I check every shoe, cupboard, and box, but they turn up nothing.

Inevitably, I end up swiping a pair of her panties from the laundry basket and kicking off my shoes as I fall into her bed. When I close my eyes, I can still see her, naked and wet and wanting. I drag the panties to my nose and unzip my jeans, fisting my cock roughly as the scenario plays through my mind. Maybe I could fuck her one last time. Taste her one last time. Wrap my fingers around the beating pulse in her throat one last time as I demand her to tell me all her secrets.

My balls contract and the muscles in my legs grow rigid as I drag my palm along the length of my cock. It's too fucking much, but it's not nearly what I want. My breath sputters as I release my pent-up frustrations across my abdomen in jets. When I collapse back onto her bed, I toss the panties onto the floor and wipe my hand on her pillow because I'm a sick fuck, and this is the only way I can be close to her.

After cleaning myself up, I move on to the other parts of the house. Again, I realize that Kat's absence hasn't much improved her life. She owns the basics but not much else. The boy's room is sparse but cozy with a twin bed and an animal theme that seems to brighten up the place. Books are scattered on the nightstand as well as a photograph of Kat and Josh together in a frame. I pick it up and stare at their faces, trying to decipher what I recognize staring back at me. His eyes and his features are familiar in a way that makes my gut churn, but I can't accept it. Not until I see proof.

Finally, in the living room closet, I hit the jackpot. There's a fireproof cabinet with hanging file folders organized into categories. I grab the one labeled Josh and do a quick scan, noting health records, daycare files, and a birth certificate. One glance at the date of his birth has me collapsing back onto the sofa in stunned silence.

He was born just a little over three years ago. Or approximately eight months after she ran from Philadelphia. The space for the father's name on the certificate is notably absent, but I don't need to see it to know the truth.

Josh is my son. And Katerina thought she could keep him from me.

THE SCHOOL IS dark and quiet as I walk down the hall leading to Kat's classroom. It's been a long day, and I'm running on little sleep. But now that I know the truth, I'm hungry for information.

A bullet to the head would have hurt less than discovering I have a son who has no idea who I am. He is half mine. Katerina and I made him together. But she took it upon herself to steal him away, never informing me of his existence.

I am all too aware of the pain of growing up without a father, so I wouldn't want that for my son. He deserves better than this. He deserves more than living a life where he doesn't know there's a man who would do anything to protect him. A man who loved him the second he became aware of the truth. It's not something I can explain or rationalize, but this changes everything.

Josh is my son. My blood. And blood is stronger than anything. Kat is about to learn what that means to me. She thinks she can run away, but there is nowhere left to hide. I've lost the first three years of his life, and I can't get those back. But I will die before I let him live a life where he doesn't know his father.

The door to Kat's classroom is locked, but it doesn't take long to find the right key on the ring of spares I had made. Once I'm inside, I take a seat at her desk and unlock the drawers, rifling through her things.

Between the erasers and pens and markers, I find little of importance. No flash drive to speak of. But there is something that catches my eye. A sticky note beneath the keyboard with an alphanumeric password scrawled across it.

Stirring her desktop computer to life, I enter the password, and sure enough, it grants me access. But after a bit of poking around, I find it isn't quite the gold mine I was hoping for either. There are no odd files lying around. Regardless, I send everything to Alexei to let him determine if anything seems suspect.

In Kat's search history, I am not surprised to see frequent searches regarding Nina's death and any updates in the case. But I am surprised to find that she has been searching my name too. Is she hoping that I'm in prison? Or is she checking up on me? That I can't say for certain, but her workspace only leaves me with more questions than answers.

I begin to tidy up her desk at first, attempting to put everything back as it was before, but then I decide against it. Maybe it's time to let Kat know she has a reason to look over her shoulder. But just in case it isn't clear, I remove the familiar pink scarf tucked inside my jacket and stuff it into her bottom drawer. A subtle message she can't miss.

Honey, I'm home.

12

KAT

I feel a slight throbbing of my head and am more tired than usual when I pull into a parking spot at the school on Friday morning. Probably the bottle of wine Luke and I shared last night at Emma's half-birthday. Guilt gnaws at me. I probably shouldn't have driven home, but I didn't want to stay.

I had no intention to drink at all, but it felt good to relax a little. Let my guard down. I've been tense all week, more than a week, and that feeling that someone's following me, watching me hasn't subsided.

Josh is humming along to a child's song from the CD we usually listen to, and when the music stops abruptly once I kill the engine, I hear his little high voice, and it makes me smile. I turn back to look at him.

"Did you and Emma have fun last night?"

"Yep. I think she liked her half-birthday gift." Josh has a crush on Emma, and it's so cute. "She can't read yet, so I read it to her," he adds casually. It was a copy of one of his favorite books, and I've read it to him so many times that he's memorized the text.

"Well, that was nice of you," I tell him. "Ready to brave the cold?"

He nods.

I open my door to slip out and can't help but glance toward the woods again.

"He's not there today, Mommy," Josh says from the back seat.

I freeze, every cell in my body icing over.

"Wh-what did you say?" I ask him finally, lifting my gaze to see his in the rearview mirror.

"The man," Josh says, pointing at the woods. "You were looking at him too."

"What man?"

"You know," he says, trying to pop the seat belt but not quite able to.

"What did he look like?"

"I don't know. He was wearing a hat and a big coat."

"When did you see him?"

He scrunches up his face. "I don't remember," he finally says.

"It's really important. Can you try to think about it?"

He nods, taps a finger to his mouth, and looks up. It's a gesture his teacher makes. He then turns back to me. "I don't remember. Can we go inside? It's cold."

I nod. "Sure, sweetie." I don't want to upset him so I try to act casual as I undo his belt and lift him out of the car.

"Are you scared of him, Mommy?" Josh asks, again surprising me. Although I guess I shouldn't be surprised. He's always been very tuned in to my feelings.

"No, dear. I just...hadn't realized you'd seen him too."

"Who is he? Is he your friend?"

I'm saved from having to answer when the bell rings. "Uh-oh, we're going to be late!" I quickly close the door, and we rush toward the front doors. I catch Josh when he slips on some ice, and he giggles.

"I'll take you skating this weekend, okay?" I tell him.

"Yay!"

The weekend coming up is a long weekend, and I'm grateful that the school's already quieter this morning. A lot of parents will take advantage of the three-day weekend and take their kids out early. Josh and I aren't going anywhere, but it'll be good to have an extra day off.

After I walk Josh into his room, I help him out of his coat and kiss him goodbye. I watch him for a moment as he rushes to his group of friends and starts playing happily.

My mind is racing as I walk out of the classroom, and I'm not paying attention when I turn the corner of the hallway to the teacher's lounge and run straight into Luke's chest.

"Whoa." His hands close around my arms, steadying me when I bounce off, and I'm reminded of another night when someone caught me like Luke just did. Steadied me. Took care of me.

I give a shake of my head. "I'm sorry, I wasn't paying attention," I tell him.

"Miss Katie, you're a klutz," Emma says with a giggle.

I force a smile at the little girl, but my anxiety is growing. "I thought you weren't going to be here today," I say to them both. Luke had told me last night he was planning to leave early to take Emma to her grandparents for a visit.

"We had to cancel," Emma says, disappointed. "Grandma doesn't feel well."

"Oh, I'm sorry to hear that," I say.

I look up at Luke. His expression is odd, and I remember last night. Remember him wanting to open another bottle and suggesting I stay over. Even offering to sleep on the couch and let me have his bed.

"Since we're around and you're around, maybe the four of us can get together again. Take the kids somewhere."

"Uh...sure." He's still holding me, so I make a point of checking my watch. "I'm going to be late."

"Oh, sorry," he says, releasing me and stepping backward.

I give an awkward wave and rush past, bypassing the teachers' lounge and heading to my office, which I share with four other teacher's aides. Our desks are divided by low partitions, and I slip my coat off, hang it on the rack by the door, and walk to the back corner where my desk is.

I'm glad no one's here yet and I can be alone. Sinking into my chair, I take a deep breath in and count as I slowly exhale, then repeat.

Josh may have been imagining seeing someone in the woods. It's not like I actually saw anyone; it was just a feeling. But then there was the feeling of being followed when I went to Daniel's Point. And all those other times this past week.

The door opens, and two of the other aides enter, talking loudly.

I force a smile and look up to find them each carrying a piece of cake and a cup of coffee.

"Good morning," I say.

"Morning, Katie," Maria and Hannah say almost simultaneously. "You'd better hurry if you want cake. It's Mr. Barnaby's birthday."

I raise my eyebrows.

"I know." Hannah giggles. "We're just as shocked as you are that he brought cake."

Mr. Barnaby is the principal and must be a hundred years old at least. And for as friendly as most of the teachers are, he's a bit of a grump.

"I'll go grab some in a minute. I just have to finish something up." I tap the keyboard to bring my computer to life and punch in my passcode. I don't have anything to finish, but I need to think. To plan. Because if it is Lev, if he's found me or if they've found me, I don't have an exit plan.

I find the folder labeled Kindie Notes and open it. Within that, I click through two more innocuously named folders before I get to the one with just a year on it. It's the year I met Lev Antonov.

Opening it, I click through into the single file there. It's password protected, and I punch in the code. The date Nina was killed. Figured I'd never forget that.

I don't know what I expect to find. Do I think it's someone from Lev's world come to take back what they wanted that night? It's not like they'd know I have it or know anything about me at all. The only person who knows I even exist is Lev, but that does little to comfort me. I know how dangerous he is. I know what he's capable of.

The day after I left, I talked to Rachel. I needed to tell her I was all right. That I was sorry for leaving like I did and that she could find the cash I'd stashed to cover my share of the rent and groceries for two months.

She told me what had happened. That Lev had turned up at the apartment soon after I left. He'd looked disheveled and smelled like fire. His clothes were dirty and spotted, and although I knew what those spots were, if she realized it, she couldn't bring herself to say it.

She told me he took my things and left and gave her money to get lost.

I haven't talked to her since, but I call her number now and again just to hear her voice and know she's safe. Know he hasn't gone after her. I never leave a message or even say hello. I don't want to put her in any danger.

I punch in the last digit of the password, and the file fills my screen.

It's a list about three pages long. A list of names. I recognize some. All have at least one date beside them. Some have a second.

Government officials, federal agents, retired and active politicians, among others. Most are powerful, connected men. Some are dead. Most of the dead men have that second date entered. The ones without that second date are mostly still living.

The dead share one thing in common. They all died tragically in some sort of accident—a car wreck, skiing accident, something random.

So, I did the math. I remember how much Nina used that term. I hated when she did. It was usually when she was annoyed with something or found something stupid.

But I did the math.

Her father stole this list from the Russian mob, and Lev was looking for it that night. Lev killed her family for this list, and my guess is it's a list of informants, of people in Vasily Stanislov's pocket.

"There you are," Janet, the older teacher with whom I work, says, startling me as she sets a piece of cake on the corner of my desk.

I fumble to close the file, and I'm sure I look guilty as sin.

If she notices, she doesn't remark, but her eyes flicker over my screen. "Isn't he growing up fast?" she says. My screensaver is a photo of Josh and me last Christmas.

"Too fast," I say.

"I snatched the last piece of cake for you," she says with a wink and sips from her mug of coffee.

"Thank you, that was thoughtful. I'll share it with Josh after lunch."

The bell rings then, and she looks up. "Well, we'd better get in there." Our classroom is connected to this office, so she goes ahead as I stand and follow her.

"Can you grab Mr. Noodle?" she asks.

"Sure."

I go back to my desk and open the bottom drawer where I keep Mr. Noodle, a sock puppet we use during story time, and my heart stops. My knees give out, and I drop into my chair. The wheels roll it slightly backward, away from the fading pink with its splatters of dark red.

I don't scream only because I can't.

Because my throat is dry, and I have no voice.

"Katie?"

I turn to find Janet peeking her head back into the office.

"Are you coming?"

I nod, touching a clammy hand to my damp forehead.

"Are you all right, dear?" she asks after seeing my face. "You look like you've seen a ghost."

"I...I don't feel well."

She comes over, reaches into the drawer and

pushes my scarf over to take the sock puppet. Does she notice the splatters of red? I'd left it in Nina's room that night. On her bed. It's her blood. And I'm going to be sick.

"Go lie down in the nurse's office. I'll be fine. We have a small room today," Janet says, and I don't answer. I just sit there staring at my scarf. The one Lev must have recognized that night. The one that he put here.

He's found me. He's here.

And my time's up.

13

KAT

As soon as the door between the office and the classroom closes, I force myself to move. To grab the scarf and shove it into my purse.

It smells like smoke. Like smoke from the fire that killed Nina. I hope to God they didn't burn her alive.

My legs tremble as I make my way out of the office, not bothering to pick up my coat as I walk out. As I concentrate on not running.

I don't pass by Josh's classroom. I'll come back for him. He's safest here with so many people around, not alone with me.

A realization comes over me then. Does Lev know about Josh? Has he seen him? Does he understand?

God.

Fuck.

Icy air forces me into the present when I open the front door and step outside. The parking lot is empty. Wind blows powder snow around. In the sunlight, it sparkles like diamond dust.

I'm going to miss it here.

I can't help but glance toward the empty woods as I make my way to my Jeep. I go to unlock the door but realize I'd never locked it this morning. I'd been too distracted with what Josh said about seeing the man.

Lev.

It has to be Lev.

But what if it's not? What if it's one of the others I saw at the club or someone else.

No. It's Lev. The scarf is proof of that.

I climb into the Jeep and start the engine, kicking myself for not having taken it to the garage yet when it takes two tries for the engine to turn over. Cold air blows at me from the vents, and I rub my hands together, freezing without my coat as I drive out of the lot and turn onto the road.

Glancing into the rearview mirror from time to time, I drive home on autopilot.

I'm going to miss our little cabin in the woods, but there's nothing to be done about it now. I have to keep us safe.

Driving faster than usual, I make it home in twenty-five minutes. I park the Jeep and look around, peering into the wooded area behind the cabin before climbing out.

He won't be hiding in the woods. Why would he?

If he's anywhere, he'll be inside.

Shit.

Shit, shit, shit.

I grab my purse, look inside for the pocketknife, and hold it in the palm of my hand. But the road is clear, and there isn't another house for a mile so unless he walked, which he can't have done with the snowfall of last week still knee-deep in the woods, he's not here.

I leave my purse in the car, just sliding my phone into my back pocket and walking toward the kitchen entrance. I peer in from the window on the door. Sunlight pours into the cozy, if a little messy, space. Josh's bowl is still sitting on the table with the blue milk from his cereal. I hate giving him that artificial stuff, but he's such a picky eater, it's just easier some mornings. I'll do better at our next place. When we start again.

Unlocking the door, I push it open to go inside, and goose bumps rise every hair on my body.

He's been here. Inside our house. I feel it now. Feel him. Smell him?

No, that's my imagination.

I quietly close the door and lean my back against it, feeling the pocketknife in my hand. I decide to switch it out for a real one and set it on the counter. My hand is trembling as I pick up another knife, a sharper one, and I don't allow myself to think about Lev. To wonder if I'll be able to do it. To kill him.

Kill him?

I grip the lip of the sink as a wave of nausea overwhelms me.

I've done it before. I know what it feels like to plunge your knife into someone's gut. I know how warm blood is when it pours over your hand. And I know how much blood there is.

But Lev?

I wipe my eyes and steel my spine. I need to get packed. I need to get our things and go.

But just then, I hear it.

Footsteps.

Fuck.

My inhale is an audible tremble matching the slow steps. He's not trying to sneak up on me.

The footsteps stop, and the hair on the back of my neck rises, the air in the room shifting, becoming heavier, making it harder to breathe.

There's a crunching sound.

"Hope you don't mind I helped myself," he says, and his voice makes my spine go rigid, makes me grip the knife so hard my knuckles go white. "And I took a shower. Fixed the leak, too."

The leaky shower drips for an hour after every shower. It drives me nuts.

"Turn around, *Katie*. Let me see you."

I'm going to be sick. I shake my head and make some strange, involuntary sound from inside my throat.

Footsteps warn me he's coming closer, then he's right behind me. I feel him, feel the warmth of his big body when he stops so close that another inch and we'd be touching, and I remember the last time he touched me.

But it's on purpose that he doesn't touch me. I know it when he brings his arms around me and brushes the crumbs off his hands in the sink and all I can do is look down at them, so big. They've been gentle, and they've been rough, but I haven't seen them be violent. Not yet. Not to me.

He leans his head close, and I close my eyes when the familiar scruff on his jaw scratches my cheek, when his fingers push my hair away from my ear, and I feel his breath tickle my neck when he speaks.

"Cat got your tongue, *Kat*."

One big hand closes around my knife hand while the other relieves me of it. I stand there, mute, and watch it clang into the sink.

"Now what were you going to do with that?"

The taunt animates me, and I thrust my elbow backward into his ribs. I don't know what I expect, but I hit a wall of solid muscle.

"Ouch," he says, and I hear the grin on his face.

I whirl, bringing both hands to his face, nails digging into his cheeks as I let out a violent scream and fight. I fight like this is the fight of my life because it is. He's going to kill me like he killed Nina. Like he killed her family and who knows how many others.

I fight even though I know I'm no match for him. He's too strong, too big, and too well trained.

I got lucky once against a predator, but Lev, he's different. Smarter. Faster.

Within a moment, he has me pressed against his chest, hand crushing my mouth to smother my scream and lifting me off my feet to carry me backward.

I kick and twist and fight every step of the way as I try to pry his arm off me, but he seems unaffected as he easily carries me through the kitchen and into the living room, then through to my bedroom where he throws me on the bed so hard I bounce twice from the force of it.

I look up at him, see the rage in his black eyes, his fisted hands, the muscles of his arms, his wide shoulders. I see the new tattoo snaking along his forearm, disappearing under the T-shirt.

His hair is still wet, and I remember he said he'd taken a shower. He's not in a hurry. He's relaxed, even. Not afraid of getting caught or of me escaping him now. Because I can't. I know it. We both know it.

He sets a knee on the bed, and I roll away.

"Get away from me!" I scream when he catches me, rolls me back, and straddles me, keeping most of his weight on his knees as he takes my arms and drags them over my head to cuff me to my own headboard.

Fuck.

He brought handcuffs?

"Let me go!"

He gets off the bed and goes to the mirror over the dresser. I watch him wipe a speck of blood off his lip. At least I managed to hurt him. But when he turns back to me, I find myself backing up away from him as much as I can, which isn't much.

"Please, Lev. Let me go. Please. I don't know anything. I didn't see anything. God, please!"

He looks down at me, and I realize how dark the room is. He's closed the curtains. Not that anyone would walk by here. There's no one for at least a mile in any direction. They won't even hear me when I scream.

He sets his knee on the edge of the bed, and I

cringe backward as he looms over me. Was he always so big?

He reaches a hand out, and I flinch, thinking he's going to hit me. But he only takes a lock of hair and lets it fall through his fingers.

"Told you your hair's prettier like this," he says.

I start to cry then. I start to sob. This is it. This is how it ends. And Josh will be alone. Who's going to bring him home? God, they can't bring him home. What if he's the one to walk in here and find what Lev leaves behind?

"Shh, Katerina." He wipes away my tears with the rough pads of his thumbs. "I don't like seeing you cry. Don't you know that?"

"Please don't hurt me. Please. I haven't told anyone anything. I haven't."

"What would you tell them? You just said you didn't see anything. That you don't know anything."

He's using my own words against me. He sits down, cocks his head to the side, and studies me. His gaze roams down over me, and I follow it, see how my blouse has come out of my jeans and my belly's exposed, see how one of my boots is gone, probably lost as I was kicking at him.

He touches my belly then, a soft touch, just his knuckles featherlight on me as he pushes the blouse a little higher. He pops the button on my jeans, and when I gasp, he spares me a glance, just a glance before returning his attention to slowly and purposely unzip my jeans.

I whimper, blubbering words that make no sense as he opens them, then pushes my panties down just a little, just enough to see the scar from my cesarean.

He traces it, and I quiet. He's gentle, just following the line back and forth and back and forth.

"Did it hurt?" he asks, never taking his eyes from it, and I realize what he's doing. He's letting me know he knows about Josh. About *our* baby.

And I start to cry again, sobs wracking my shoulders.

Lev returns his attention to my face, leaving the scar and watching me, eyes hard and angry.

"Katerina, Katerina, Katerina. What am I going to do with you?"

14

LEV

She shivers beneath my touch, and I can't help myself. I know she's afraid of me. I know she's fucking terrified right now, but it's been so long since I've tasted her. When I lean down and squeeze her jaw between my fingers to hold her in place, she freezes, and I drag my lips over hers.

She bucks against me, and a choked sound escapes her before she starts pleading again. "Lev."

The salt of her tears tangles with the blood on my lip, and it produces a violent want in me. I could cut the clothes from her body right now and squeeze my cock inside her. A punishment for trying to take this away from me.

"Don't you know this belongs to me?" My thumb digs into the pulsing vein in her throat, the very life-force of her being. I want her to know there's no escaping me. In life or in death, I will follow her.

"Lev, please." Her chest heaves as she shakes her head. "My son needs me."

"Our son," I snarl. "He's our fucking son, Katerina. Will you deny it?"

She bites her lip as more tears spill onto her cheeks. "He needs his mother."

"And what about his father?" I drag my fingers away from her face and stare into her eyes. "You are content to let him believe he has none? You are content to take what is half mine from me?"

"You're the fucking mob!" she cries out. "You killed Nina and her family! What choice did you leave me with?"

And this is what it all boils down to. I knew the day would come when we would need to have this conversation. Kat has had four years to ruminate on the events of that night. In her mind, she has already tried and convicted me. The only defense I have is my word, and I don't know that she'll ever trust me enough to believe me. Regardless, it doesn't matter. She's chained herself to me for life now. That just hasn't sunk in for her yet.

"I didn't kill Nina or her mother." I force her gaze back to mine when she tries to turn away. "I did kill William. That was the only reason I went there that day."

"I saw your car," she whispers. "I know it was you."

"Did you see me shoot them?" I challenge.

"No, but—"

"You saw my car, but you didn't see what happened. Everything else... all the decisions you made after that were based on an assumption. Your assumption was wrong."

"I'm not wrong." Her lip quivers. "You put the scarf in the desk to taunt me. It still has her blood on it."

I brush away her tears with my thumbs and smooth the hair away from her face. She is so fucking beautiful. I remember when she looked at me like I was her hero. Now, I'm the enemy, and it feels like a betrayal. A hot knife in my back. I don't know how to make her understand.

"Do you think I took enjoyment in what happened to your friend?" I ask her. "Is that really your opinion of me?"

She hesitates, her brows pinching together in confusion. It only lasts a moment, but that uncertainty is there. She just isn't willing to admit it.

"Do you want to know what I think, Katya?" I graze the length of her arm with my palm. "I think you continue to tell yourself this story so you can hate me. So you can feel better about what you did."

"What I did?" She glares up at me. "Are you seriously trying to tell me I'm the one in the wrong here?"

"You ran from me without waiting for an explanation. You took my child. And for four goddamn years, you left me to wonder if you were safe."

Her eyes cloud with emotions, too many to recognize. She still wants to keep her secrets, but Kat will come to understand there can be no more lies between us.

"You said you were done with me," she reminds me. "That I'd never see you again."

"I came for you," I tell her. "I came to protect you."

"Or to kill me," she supplies.

"Don't you think if that's what I wanted, it would already be done?"

She doesn't answer, and the room falls silent. The truth is, she isn't going to trust me. But her trust is irrelevant right now. Perhaps it is time to show my hand.

"Let me tell you how this is going to go." I stand and drag the phone from my pocket when it signals another text. Vasily is losing his fucking patience as far as I'm concerned. It's a problem I will need to contend with sooner rather than later.

"That drive you have stored on your computer at school?" I stuff my phone in my pocket and return my attention to Kat. "It's going to disappear. Tonight."

She blinks, her features pinching with frustration as she realizes the only source of protection she had against me is worthless now.

"It's time to cut the bullshit," I continue. "We're going to have an earnest discussion about your past. I want to hear it from your lips. The truth. No more secrets. Keep in mind I already know a great deal about you, so if you're thinking about lying to me, you may want to consider that."

"Why does my past matter?" she bites back.

"Because I want to know you."

My words shatter the anger in her eyes, but only for a second.

"Lev, this is crazy. You can't just come in here and tell me what to do. That's not how life works."

"I live in a different world, sweetheart. And now, you do too."

"What does that mean?" she demands.

"It means we have a child together, and if you think for one second you're taking him away from me now, you're delusional."

"So, what then?" Her voice rises. "You're just going to keep me chained to the bed and demand I do whatever you say? Is that it?"

Her attitude makes my cock twitch, and despite the seriousness of the conversation, my lip is already tilting up into a smirk. "I don't see a problem with that idea."

"This isn't a joke," she hisses. "I have a job. Responsibilities. Josh has school and his friends..."

"Your job doesn't matter anymore. I'm here to take care of you now. I'm going to take care of both of you. Josh will have everything he needs and more."

"Are you trying to tell me...?" She stumbles over the words. "Do you think you're going to live with us?"

"Well, I sure as fuck can't let you out of my sight, now can I?" I narrow my eyes at her. "You'd run the first chance you got, and then I'd have to track you down and do this all over again. As much fun as I've had hunting you, this game has grown tiresome, Kat. You're caught. That's it. It's time to accept it."

"You're insane." She shakes her head.

I lean down into her face, my lips a whisper away from hers. "Only because you make me so."

She closes her eyes and shivers, and I wrap my fist with her hair as I drink from her lips again. This time, the fight has gone out of her, and as much as she might want to declare me a monster, her body says otherwise.

"I bet if I were to drag my fingers through your pussy right now, you'd be soaked for me."

She shakes her head, her lips too weak to deny it. But it doesn't matter because I can smell her arousal.

I grind my dick against her hip, and she makes a sound in her throat that tempts me beyond reason.

"Tell me you haven't thought of this," I whisper into her ear. "Tell me you haven't missed this."

"I haven't," she lies through her teeth. "In fact, I have a boyfriend now."

"Who? That fuckface Luke?" I bite her neck, and she freezes at the mention of his name. "Yeah, nice try, sweetheart. I know you don't spread your legs for him. It would be hard for you, considering you could only ever think of me."

I wait for her protest, but it doesn't come. And the notion that I might be right has me so goddamned hard I could fuck her for two days straight and never be satisfied. My fingers slip down between her jeans and panties, and she shakes her head, suddenly frantic.

"Not while I'm handcuffed. Please, Lev."

When I glance at her face, the fear there is real. And it's enough to douse me with cold water. I drag my hand out of her jeans and force her chin up, so she has to look at me.

"Tell me why."

"I'm afraid you're going to hurt me." Her body shakes under the weight of her confession, and it kills me.

"Then don't make me." I unlock the handcuffs

and rub her wrists before I lie down beside her and tug her against my body.

For a second, she doesn't move or even breathe. But when I wrap my arm around her waist and bury my face in her hair to inhale her, she finally lets some of the tension bleed from her body.

15

KAT

I close my eyes, and for the first time in four years, I feel myself relax. A tear slides over the bridge of my nose and drops onto the bed, and I give myself over to it, to letting go. It's just for a minute, I tell myself. Just one minute.

Lev can't be a part of Josh's life. He's a mobster. Him being in Josh's life means Josh becomes a part of that world, even if Lev doesn't want that, and I'm not sure what he wants. It just can't happen.

But for one minute, I can let him hold me. I just need this little sliver of time.

He feels good at my back. Solid. And part of me wishes I could stay. Could let him stay.

All my life, I've relied on myself. I don't remember my mother. I have nothing of hers, not a single photo, not one thing to even pretend I remember. To create a memory. I remember my first years in foster care, though. And the ones that followed and got progressively worse.

I was a throwaway kid. Not one person gave a single damn about me. That's why I ended up in juvenile detention when they knew who was truly guilty. When they knew what Robert George was doing and would continue to do if I hadn't sunk that knife into his gut.

But I guess sealing my records was enough to alleviate their guilt of locking me up.

Not that it mattered. Another home or detention. At least in detention I didn't have to pretend. I was treated like a criminal, but at least I was left alone. No one fucked with me there. Not the guards and not the other kids.

But that's all past and feeling Lev behind me now, feeling his strong arm tighten around my middle, I know he can keep me safe. And he may even want to. Or think he wants to.

If Josh wasn't in the picture, would he want to then, I wonder. But I don't let myself go down that road. Instead, I have to think about Josh.

I feel Lev's body relax behind me. He's not gripping me.

If I'm quick, I can get out. Knock him out long enough to get back to the school, get Josh, and get out.

Josh will be upset not to have his things, but I'll fix that later. I have no choice because I can't allow the alternative.

"I need to use the bathroom." I roll backward a little, and my belly quivers at the feel of him behind me. It's like my body remembers. And I think about something. About when we were together.

I used to come when Mr. George touched me. When he forced me. I felt sick about it, but I did. And he loved it. Loved rubbing my face in it. Loved that Joshua saw me come again and again. Saw me enjoy the very thing that revolted me. That had me puking my guts out after it was over.

But when I was with Lev, it was different.

It was beautiful.

Fuck.

He pulls his arm away, and I press the heels of my hands into my eyes. They come away wet, and when I look at him, he isn't surprised or upset I guess that I'm still wiping away tears.

I sit up and swing my legs over the edge of the bed.

Lev stands, and I look up at him on the other side of the bed.

He's beautiful in a cruel sort of way. When he's not smiling, there's something dark about him. But when he smiles, and he does just now, I see that dimple. And just as Josh's smile reminds me of Lev, Lev's reminds me of Josh.

And that's what I need to think about now. Josh is who I need to think about.

Lev walks around the bed and takes my arm. He leans down, and I look up. His face is only inches from mine. He squeezes my arm a little. It doesn't hurt, but I know it can hurt. I know he can make it hurt. He's warning me.

"Don't try anything stupid, understand?"

Can he read my mind?

I blink fast, and it takes all I have not to look away, but I know if I do, he'll see I'm lying. So instead, I nod, swallowing back my anxiety.

I have one shot at this. And if I fail...no, I can't think about that. I can't fail.

He releases me, gestures to the bathroom with a jerk of his head, and slips his phone out of his back pocket.

I walk awkwardly with just the one boot on into the bathroom. I have to remember to grab the other one when I leave.

I'm closing the door when Lev calls my name.

"Kat."

I stop and peer out.

"Don't lock it."

I slip back and close the door. The lock is one of those push-button locks anyway, and I'm sure he could break that without much effort, so it's not a big deal to leave it unlocked.

I turn to the sink and meet my reflection. My face is blotchy, my eyes puffy and red from crying. I turn the tap and cup a handful of cold water to splash on my face. I keep it running as I bend down and open the cabinet beneath the sink. I know when it will creak so I'm careful to stop just before. I reach my arm inside and twist my body so I can reach around behind the pipes.

There, taped to the top of the cabinet, I feel the hard metal of the pistol I purchased illegally four years ago. Two nights after I ran.

I practiced with it that year I was pregnant, but I haven't touched it since Josh was born. I hate the thing, and even now, taking the cold, hard pistol in the palm of my hand, as small as it is, I feel its power, and I know the damage it can do. The havoc it will wreak.

But I have no choice.

I straighten. It's loaded. Six bullets. So, I guess I have six chances, not one.

"Kat?" Lev calls from the other side of the door.

"Just a sec," I say, flushing the toilet and taking a deep breath. I flex my hand around the pistol, stare straight ahead at the door and cock the gun.

Then I open the door.

Lev's a few feet away. He looks up as he finishes

typing the last of his text and tucks the phone into his pocket. I think that all happens in just a split second of time. It just feels like it's stretched out to me.

When I lift my arm, it feels like slow motion. His expression changes, darkening as I raise the gun and aim it at him.

I don't have to shoot him.

I don't want to hurt him.

Maybe I can make him cuff himself to the bed. Maybe I can do that.

Lev's eyes narrow. He looks disappointed first, then angry as his mouth tightens into a thin, hard line.

"I don't want to hurt you," I hear myself say, and my voice sounds strange, as though I'm in a tunnel. I'm crying again. I feel the tears, and my hand is shaking, and I have to shoot. I have to.

"Put it down, Kat."

I shake my head.

He takes a step toward me.

I take one back. I need to shoot. Now. I need to pull that damned trigger.

"Handcuff yourself to the bed," I try, my voice trembling. Weak.

He takes another step. I'm almost out of space.

"I'll shoot. I mean it."

My back touches the wall. I didn't realize I was

still backing up. But Lev keeps coming, taking that last step until he's pressing his chest into the barrel of the gun, leaning into it.

"No, you won't."

"Please," I sob. I'm the one with the gun, yet I'm pleading with him.

He cocks his head, eyes matching the cold steel of the weapon. He closes his big hand over mine, and I have no choice. I have to do this. I have to shoot.

And I do.

I pull the trigger.

The sound isn't like the night at Nina's. That popping was quieter. This shot, it's loud. And we're both falling.

As we go down, Lev shifts his position, changing his grip of my gun hand to my wrist, aiming it over my head.

Another shot goes off, and I hear myself scream as glass shatters somewhere behind me.

His other hand comes around to cup the back of my head just as I hit the floor, the wood hard as I slam into it with his weight on top of me.

I'm not sure if it's the force of the fall or his grip on my wrist that has my hand opening, but the gun slides across the floor and under the bed. I watch it, then turn to him. I should see blood. I shot him.

Didn't I?

But there's no blood, and Lev isn't hurt. He's just really, really pissed.

He takes my jaw and squeezes so hard I think he's going to break it. "Didn't I tell you not to do anything stupid?" he asks through gritted teeth.

I claw at his forearm, feeling his skin under my fingernails. Instinct takes over, and I ram my knee up into his balls.

Lev curses, and it's only then that I can move.

I flip over onto my belly, and I clamber toward the bed, trying to drag my legs out from under him, but he grips the waistband of my jeans and hauls me backward. Standing, he lifts me with him. He's still cursing, still not quite upright after my assault on his balls.

He tosses me on the bed again, laying all his weight over me so I'm trapped. He pushes the hair away from my face, and his breath is warm on my cheek.

"Didn't I fucking tell you not to do anything stupid?" His hand slides between us, and he's fumbling with something. "And that was about as stupid as it gets."

He straightens, and I start to, too, but he shoves me back down, jamming his knee into my lower back.

I can't move more than a few inches, and I crane

my neck to look back at him, and I see what he's fumbling with. What he's opening.

"Lev, no," I plead as he unbuckles his belt. I claw at the bed, trying to drag myself away, but it's hopeless.

"Kat, yes," he says, mimicking me as his hands slide between the bed and my belly. I fight and twist and turn to get away, but I can't. He's too strong. And when he tugs my jeans down, I scream.

His fingers are in my hair, hauling me backward against him. Looking around, he finds a scarf I'd tossed over the back of the chair and drags me with him as he picks it up. He squeezes his fingers and makes me look at him. He's a blur through my tears.

"You made me do this. You brought this on yourself."

"Lev—"

But before I can finish, he has me back over the bed and ties the scarf over my mouth, and when I open it to scream or to plead, he tightens it. Then he finishes stripping me of my underwear so they and my jeans are down around my knees, and I think he's going to do it. Do *that*.

Everything stops for a minute then. Or maybe it's a split second. It gets quiet and perfectly still, and the only sound is my breathing, my pleading through that gag. I turn my head to find him looking at me.

"I don't like hurting you, Katerina," he says.

I want to tell him not to, that he doesn't have to, but I'm gagged. He tugs his belt through the loops of his jeans and doubles it over. When I understand what he intends to do, another panic, a different sort of panic takes hold of me.

I shake my head, and when I try to claw against the bed to get away, he takes his knee off my back, captures my wrists, and holds them at my lower back.

"But you have to learn this lesson, and you have to learn it now."

I watch in shock as he raises his arm and brings it down hard.

Silence after that reverberating sound of leather against flesh. Silence as it echoes, and my breath catches as fire slices through me.

"You will do as I say." He lashes me again, holding me still when I fight to get away. "You will do exactly as you're told."

He strikes again and again and again, and it's too fast, and I don't have time to catch my breath or process as pain sears my ass and thighs.

I'm sobbing, the scarf-gag is drenched, and he's not done yet. Not even when I lose count. Only when I stop fighting, only when my body droops onto the bed, and I take it, take his punishment does he finally stop. Only then do I finally hear the clang of the belt buckle as it lands on the floor, and my wrists are free, and I feel myself slide down over the edge of the bed to my knees, my hands still behind me as if he's still holding them.

I press my face into the blanket and sob and I feel him behind me, feel him kneel at my back. He's close enough that I can feel his hardness.

He's aroused.

Whipping me aroused him.

I make a sound into the gag, into the blanket because if this isn't over, if he touches me now, I'll die. I will die.

But then the gag is gone, and he cups the back of my head, and when he turns my face into his chest, I let him.

"I don't like hurting you," he says, and his voice is choked and tight.

I hear his heart. Listen to the rapid beating against his warm chest.

He's rubbing my punished ass, and his touch is soft, so opposite of the violence of moments ago. But this is him, isn't it? The dichotomy of Lev.

Violence and tenderness, they're interchangeable.

He is capable of both to an extreme.

He sits on the floor beside me, pulls my underwear and jeans up, then tugs me into his lap. I rub my face and wipe my nose with my sleeve.

I look up at him, and he's watching me with sad eyes, not angry ones, not anymore.

Without a word, he wipes my face, pushes the hair that's sticking to my face back and he kisses my forehead, kisses the lids of my eyes when I close them. Kisses my cheeks, then my mouth and I hate myself for not fighting him. For not wanting him to stop.

16

LEV

"What are you doing?" she whispers as I assault her throat with my lips.

"I'm taking back what's mine," I murmur against her. "Get used to it."

"You hurt me." She sniffs.

"Did I?" I mock her. "What did you suppose would happen when you pulled that trigger, Katya? Were you prepared to watch my blood splatter across your bedroom floor?"

"I didn't want to do it." She squeezes her eyes shut and shakes her head. "You forced my hand."

"And now you've forced mine," I echo.

"You repeatedly told me you were bad for me," she reminds me. "You warned me away. And now you're here holding me hostage like this is exactly what you wanted all along."

"This is the last thing I wanted for you," I tell her. "And I meant everything I said before. But that doesn't mean I didn't want it. You were supposed to forget me and have a normal life. And maybe I would have actually let you, who the fuck knows. Regardless of that, we have a kid now. Whatever intentions I may have had in the past are irrelevant in the face of that. Like it or not, Kat, you've chained yourself to me for life now."

Her body quakes in silent grief as she curls into herself, accepting the facts she can't deny. She may not like the truth, but I'm done handling her with kid gloves.

"You don't get to kill me," I murmur against her. "You don't get to leave me again."

She doesn't respond. All of her fight has abandoned her, and she will remember this day every time she sits down for the next week. Still, when I take the opportunity to reacquaint myself with her body, she doesn't protest. Touching her curves, breathing her in, tasting the salt of her skin. And this time, when I slip my fingers between her thighs and rub her through her jeans, she whimpers.

"Did you miss this?" I ask her roughly. "Did you miss my hands on your body?"

She doesn't answer, but her body is doing enough talking. Her nipples are so hard they are scraping against the thin fabric of her shirt. And between her legs, her jeans are damp with want.

"Tell me you hate it." I bite at her collarbone as my other hand palms her breast. "But only if you mean it."

Again, she doesn't answer. And this time, when I unzip her jeans and slip my fingers between her thighs, there's no denying she's soaked for me.

"I can't tell you what this does to me." I bury two fingers into her wetness, and she jerks against the intrusion.

"Lev..." She closes her eyes and bites her lip as she tries to come up with another protest. But her thought goes unfinished as I torture her slowly, grinding my cock against her ass as my fingers thrust into her pussy. She's trying not to make a sound, not to show how much she needs this right now, but I can feel it in her every breath.

"Kiss me," I demand as my lips settle over hers.

She tries not to, but for one split second, she caves, and her lips part, allowing me access to her mouth. I slide my tongue against hers, and she lets out the softest of sounds as her hips buck against my hand. I'm fingering her now. Assaulting her with my lips and teeth and thumb. She closes her eyes as every muscle in her body tenses. She doesn't want to give in, but it's a foolish notion.

"Quit fighting it," I growl, yanking my fingers from her pussy and bringing them to her lips.

Her eyes widen in shock when I force them into her mouth.

"Taste your want for me." I smirk. "Tell me how much you don't like it."

"Fuck you," she hisses, turning away and smearing her arousal across her cheek.

Darkness overtakes my features as I look down on her.

"Fuck me?" I slowly unzip my jeans, and she squirms beneath me. "All you had to do was ask."

"Lev." Her voice betrays her nerves as I reach for her hand and bring it to my throbbing cock.

"Stroke me." My fingers return to her pussy as she stares up at me, eyes ablaze with equal fire and hatred.

When she squeezes my cock in her grasp, she means to hurt me, but it only makes me harder.

"Remember the rules." I glare at her as I thrust my fingers back inside her. "You hurt me, I hurt you."

"I don't like your rules," she protests weakly.

"But you like my fingers inside you." I observe pointedly. "Now be good and stroke my cock."

It takes her some time, but when the tension starts to build again in her body, she's gripping me with an iron fist, dragging her palm up and down my shaft like her life depends on it. I'm not delusional enough to believe she's doing it out of her goodwill. She just doesn't want me to stop making her feel good.

"Don't come," I warn her when she squeezes around my fingers. "Not yet."

She shakes her head, panting, jerking her body against me. "I...I can't—"

When she reaches the edge of the cliff, I withdraw from her body, and she stares up at me in horror. I want to hear her beg, but her pride won't allow it. Not just yet.

"You want to come?" I ask her.

She glares at me as I shove my jeans down to my knees and roll on top of her.

"Answer me." I squeeze her face in my grasp. "Do you want to come?"

"You started this." She hurls the words out like a brat.

"And now I'm going to finish it." I drag the fat head of my cock against her slickness, and her nails curl into my biceps. Thrusting my hips forward, I bury myself inside her until she can't take any more of my length.

"Fuuuuck." I groan into her neck as I roll my hips and slam into her again. She is so goddamn tight. It's been four long years, and I'm not going to last.

"Now you can come." I fist a handful of her hair

and force her to look up at me. "But only if you come around my cock."

She whimpers as I fuck her into the floor. Her nails claw at my back. My eyes roll back in my head. I can't fucking concentrate. I just need to fuck her.

When Kat finally lets herself go, an agonized groan escapes between her lips. I swallow it whole, and then drink from her until she's breathless and her lips are swollen from my kiss. Then she fucking bites me, tearing at my lip until I taste my own blood. When I rear back, she adds insult to injury by slapping me as hard as she can manage.

"I hate you!" she screams.

My fingers wrap around her throat, and she shrinks back into the floor. "Is that how you want to play?"

"I didn't mean to!" She tosses out a half-assed apology as I flip her over onto all fours and shove her face down into the carpet.

I squeeze the delicate flesh around her throat, forcing her to arch back as I thrust my wet dick inside her. She whines when I reach between her legs and start toying with her overly sensitive clit.

She shakes her head, panting as she tries to pry my fingers away, but I don't fucking budge. Fingering her until she's screaming is my new favorite pastime. The sound of my flesh slapping against hers reverberates off the walls as I force my cock in and out of her. She cries out in agony as she comes again, and then squeals when I lay my entire body over hers, sinking my teeth into her shoulder.

I dig my fingers into her hips and thrust into her one last time, my cock unleashing four years of pent-up tension and a fuck load of cum.

Dragging her down with me, we collapse into a heap on the floor with my dick still inside her. Kat gasps when she feels the sticky mess between her thighs.

"I'm not on birth control," she screeches.

"I know." I bury my face into her neck with a contented sigh and close my eyes.

"You know?" she repeats.

"You're mine." My cock twitches inside her. "And if I want to fuck you raw, I will."

"And if I get pregnant again?" she croaks.

"Then Josh gets a little brother."

The air deflates from her chest, and she stares at me like I'm insane before her eyes drift to my lips. I wipe the blood away with my thumb and push it between her lips, smearing it across her teeth. And then I kiss her again. She parts her lips for me, and I drink from her until she's tapping my arm in a silent plea to come up for air.

"Did you let anyone else touch you this way while I was gone?" I ask when I pull away.

"No," she whispers as she stares up at the ceiling.

"Good girl." I pet her hair and kiss her forehead.

We lay together in silence for another hour. I hold her close, refusing any distance between us, until inevitably, she gives up the last of her resistance and closes her eyes. She's exhausted, but there isn't time to sleep.

When I finally pull out of her and tug my jeans back up, she looks at me in question.

"Come on." I hold my hand out to help her up. "We need to get cleaned up so we can go pick up Josh."

At the mention of his name, she doesn't hesitate to do as she's asked. Whatever fire may have lingered in her earlier is nothing but smoldering ash as I lead her into the bathroom and turn on the shower.

Kat frowns as I remove the rest of her clothes, repeating the process on myself. She tries to cover herself up, hiding her old scars and the new one. The scar across her belly from when our son came into this world.

"Don't hide from me." I reach out and touch her there again. "This is nothing to be ashamed of. Someday soon, I want to know about his birth. I want to know all of it."

She swallows, and I open the shower door, urging her inside. Together, we stand under the spray, and she shivers as I wash her body, taking extra care between her thighs and the welted red marks on her ass. It obviously stings, and she sucks in a breath every time I touch one of the marks, but she doesn't tell me to stop.

Even though she showered this morning, I wash her hair again and comb it away from her face with my fingers before I tug her against my body and kiss her neck. She melts into me, and for a while, we just stand there, until the spray of the shower goes cold, forcing us to evacuate.

I towel her off and brush her hair as she stands before me, numb and silent. She's trapped inside her own mind right now and asking her to function would be too much. So I take on the burden without regret, smearing some aloe lotion into the welt marks on her ass and dressing her again. After I've dried her hair and secured it with an elastic band, I remove my own towel and dress myself as her eyes rake over my body, pausing briefly on my cock before her cheeks flush and she turns away.

"It's okay." I smile behind her. "You can look at it if you want."

She clears her throat and crosses her arms as I rifle through her closet and find another jacket. She seems confused by the gesture until I remind her that she left her other one at school.

The nerves return to her face, and when she reaches for the jacket, I don't let it go just yet.

"I'm sure I don't have to tell you this, Katerina.

You're a smart woman. But if you think about making a scene at the school, or anywhere else, you may want to consider how far Vasily's influence stretches."

"What does that mean?" she asks.

"That list of names on the drive?" I return her gaze. "That was just one of many. Cops, politicians, government employees. They can all be bought, or they can disappear. The moral of the story is that without me, there isn't a place on this earth you'll be safe. It's something to think about."

Her jaw flexes, but she nods her understanding. I release the jacket, and she slips it on.

"What am I supposed to say if someone asks who you are?" she questions.

"Tell them I'm an old friend. The same for Josh. At least until he's had some time to get to know me. Then we can tell him the truth. Together."

Kat frowns and doesn't respond. Together, we walk out of the house, and I lock the door with the spare set of keys from my pocket. She stares at me in disbelief as I lead her around to the passenger seat of her Jeep and secure her seat belt. Just like old times. When my arm brushes hers, she looks away, but it doesn't change the fact that she still shivered like it was the first time.

The Jeep takes three attempts to start, and it

bothers me that she's been driving this piece of shit around like this.

"I've been meaning to get it fixed." She stares out the window.

"I'll take care of it."

I pull out of the driveway and turn onto the main road. Kat doesn't bother to give me directions. By now, she's aware I don't need them. The chatter from the radio is the only sound between us, and I don't like it.

"Can you just tell me one thing?" she croaks.

I glance at her across the seat. "What?"

"Did Nina suffer?"

My fingers tighten around the steering wheel as I consider how much to tell her. I meant what I said about honesty earlier, and I know that goes both ways. It might hurt her to hear the truth, but if I expect the same from her, I won't be a hypocrite.

"I know she put up a fight," I admit. "She bit the man who was there with me. I was downstairs, and I didn't see it happen. But it happened quickly. Five, maybe ten minutes. He shot her before I could get to her."

Kat releases a painful sob and more tears begin to spill down her cheeks before I reach over and touch her arm.

"I am sorry, Katya. I'm sorry that I couldn't save her."

She squeezes her eyes shut and shakes her head. "I should have taken her with me."

"It isn't your fault," I assure her.

We pull into the parking lot of the school, and I kill the engine and turn to her, wiping away the evidence of her tears.

"No more tears today," I say. "Josh wouldn't like to see his mother upset."

At this, she nods, attempting to gather herself together as she pulls down the visor and looks at her reflection in the mirror. "I'm a mess."

She digs through her purse and finds a compact, which she uses to dab her face with powder. After a couple of minutes, she grumbles that it will have to do and shuts the visor. I walk around to help her from the car, and it happens naturally that we fall back into this rhythm. She waits for me and doesn't protest when I place my hand against her back, but I wonder if she's considering my warning as we walk inside the building.

"We still have a few minutes," I inform her. "Let's go to your desk first."

Her shoulders tense, but she allows me to lead her in the direction of her room. She goes through the process of unlocking the door and smiles at another teacher as they walk down the hall.

But once we're inside and the door shut behind us, she seems less certain. I don't doubt that she's still weighing her options, but she is too smart to disregard what I told her earlier.

"Log in to your computer." I gesture to the chair in front of the desk.

She sighs and takes a seat, reaching for the mouse. But instead of stirring the screen to life, it loads to a blue screen.

"What the...?" Her words drift off as it occurs to her what's happening. Alexei has already come through as promised.

"Everything is gone," I inform her. "Just in case you doubted what I told you earlier."

The bell rings before she can speak, and I gesture her toward the door.

"Come. Let's go see our son."

JOSH GLANCES up at me with a curious expression and eyes so much like my own it hurts to breathe. *My son.*

"Who is this, Mommy?" Josh asks.

"He's a friend." Kat offers him a watery smile as she watches our exchange take place. "His name is Lev."

"Lev," Josh repeats.

I kneel before him and resist the natural instinct to pull him into my arms. He doesn't know me. A fact that's still difficult to swallow. We just need some time.

"Hey, buddy." I offer him a pained smile. "How was your day?"

"Good." He shrugs before looking at Kat. "Mommy, can we get pizza?"

Her expression tightens when she looks at me.

"I like pizza," I tell him. "What's your favorite?"

"Pepperoni," he chants triumphantly.

"He likes the Village Pizza shop," Kat explains. "It's his favorite."

"Village Pizza it is then." I wink at Josh. "How about a lift?"

He flashes a dimple at me and nods enthusiastically before I throw him up onto my shoulders. Kat looks like she's going to have a heart attack as we walk out of the school like that, and her face pales completely when we run into douchebag Luke on the way out.

"Hey, Katie." His smile fades as his eyes roam over me and Josh beside her.

"Hi, Luke." She forces the words through stiff lips. "I'm sorry, I can't really talk right now. We're on our way out to dinner."

His eyes narrow in my direction, and I smirk. That's right, asshole. *My family.*

"Are we still on for this weekend?" he asks.

"Uh..." She shifts her feet and stares off into the distance.

"Katie's busy this weekend," I answer for her. "And every weekend for the foreseeable future."

Her mouth falls open as she glares at me, and Luke looks like he's tempted to challenge my assertion. Something that won't end well for him.

"C'mon, *Katie*." I press my palm against her lower back and urge her forward. "Josh is hungry."

Luke stands there like a fucking moron, gaping at us as we leave him behind. Only once we're out of earshot does she whisper under her breath.

"You didn't have to be such a dick to him."

"I wanted to get my point across." I hoist Josh down from my shoulders and into his car seat. But when it comes to buckling him in, that's where I realize I'm fucking lost.

"Here." Kat shoves me out of the way. "You have to do it a certain way."

I watch over her shoulder as she secures him into the seat, tugging on the straps until they are snug. It might be a little issue, but it feels like a big fucking deal to me. I should know how to do this.

I'm trapped inside my own thoughts as I open the door for Kat and buckle her in. At least that much I can do. When I start the Jeep, she gives me directions to the pizza place. It's still early, but neither of us has eaten since this morning anyway.

When I pull into the lot and cut the engine, she turns to me. "Should we order it to go?"

"Noooo!" Josh protests. "I want to play games!"

I shrug. "Sounds like the boy wants to play some games."

Kat doesn't look as sold on the idea, and I can tell she's still nervous. She feels protective of Josh as a good mother should. But she needs to come to an understanding that the last person she needs to protect him from is me.

Inside, the waitress seats us and takes our order. Josh can hardly sit still long enough to tell her he wants pepperoni pizza before he's begging to go play some games.

"How about after dinner?" She tries to reason with him.

"I'll take him." I stand and hold out my hand for his, and to my relief, he takes it. Kat scrambles out of the booth behind us and follows us to the Whac-A-Mole game. I throw in a few quarters, and Josh giggles as he tries to squash the moles.

"You can't just undermine whatever I say," she whispers while he's distracted. "It will make him think he doesn't have to listen to me."

"Relax." I reach between us and squeeze her hand. "It's my first day. I just want him to have fun."

Her expression softens a fraction, and she nods

in understanding. "Okay, but let's not make it a habit."

Josh finishes the game and then bolts toward another one. We find a few that I can actually play with him, and he gets a real kick out of it when he actually beats me. The sacrifice of my pride is worth every giggle. By the time we eat our pizza and have another round of games, Kat informs me it's almost his bedtime.

"Already?" I glance at my phone.

"He's only three," she says. "He has a routine, and I don't want to disrupt that."

I nod. "Alright, buddy. You heard your mom. Time to go."

Josh pouts but does as he's told. Kat helps him into his coat, and I pay the bill before we head back to her house. When we get there, she goes about the process of his nightly routine, which I discover is a bath and brushing his teeth before he hops into bed.

"Ready for story time?" she asks.

He nods with a yawn, and I lean against the doorframe in his room. "Mind if I read tonight?"

Kat hesitates, glancing at the book in her hands. "Would that be okay, Josh?"

Josh smiles, and I settle next to Kat on the bed, my leg brushing against hers when she hands me the book. She glances down between us but doesn't move away as I expected she might.

"I hope you're good at voices," she says with an attempt at levity. "Josh likes his stories pretty animated."

"I think I can make it work." I wink at him as I turn to the first page. "Now let's see about these gorillas."

17

KAT

I leave Lev to read but stand just outside the bedroom listening as he makes all the sounds of the different characters. In spite of myself, I have to smile at some of them, and hearing Josh giggle is what triggers it.

He won't hurt Josh, and I know that. I'm not afraid of that at all, actually. But there is another thought niggling at me. Would he try to take Josh away from me?

Just the thought makes me shudder, and I hug my arms to myself. I walk into the kitchen and put the kettle on to make tea. Past my reflection in the window, a flurry of snow falls to the ground. I'm not sure if it's the wind rustling up the already fallen snow or if it's the next front that's predicted.

I focus on my face in the glass. I look pale and tired.

The kettle whistles, startling me. I hurry to take it off the flame and set it on the back burner while spooning loose jasmine green tea into a tea bag. Setting that into the teapot Josh and I painted together at the local ceramic shop, I pour hot water over it.

When I next look up, my face isn't the only one in the window.

My breath catches as I turn, and I meet Lev's eyes. The cabin isn't big, it's just right for Josh and me, but with Lev here, it looks tiny. Like a dollhouse. He's a hulking figure in the kitchen, and just his size alone makes my belly flip. I don't want to want this. Want him. Didn't the violence of the afternoon prove to me how bad he is for me? For us?

But I can't deny that being near him does something to me.

"He's a sweet kid," Lev says, pulling out a chair and taking a seat. "You did good."

I'm surprised by the compliment. Not that I think I've done badly with Josh, but just that he's saying that.

"Thanks," I say, busying myself with taking out the tea bag. It should steep longer, but I don't know what to do with my hands. "Tea?" I ask when I turn around.

"Do you have something stronger?"

"Um…" I look around the kitchen, then remember the almost-full bottle of vodka in the freezer. Luke had brought it a long time ago. I can't even remember the occasion because I don't drink much in general. "Here," I say, taking it out, deciding not to mention it's from Luke.

He takes the bottle and reads the label. "It'll do, but we'll get some good stuff tomorrow."

"I don't really drink. There's no need."

"I do drink," he says. Is that his way of telling me he's staying?

I get him a glass. "Do you want ice?"

He shakes his head. "It's cold enough."

I stand there, not quite sure what to do.

"Sit down, Katerina."

"Why? Do I make you nervous with all these sharp knives around?"

His lips curl upward. "I can repeat this afternoon's lesson if you need me to." He pushes the chair out with his foot. "Sit."

I sit, wincing when my butt hits the wooden chair. If he notices, and I'm sure he does, he doesn't comment. Instead, he pours himself two fingers of vodka. I consider getting up to get a cushion but don't want to give him the satisfaction.

"You can't stay here," I say, pouring myself a cup of tea.

"I thought I made it clear that's not up for discussion."

"Where will you sleep?"

He just raises his eyebrows and swallows back the vodka.

"What will I tell Josh? How do I explain my 'friend' is sleeping in my bed?"

"We'll figure that out. We have more important things to discuss."

Yes, I know we do. If Lev found me, and his friend or whoever erased my hard drive from wherever he is found me, who else knows I'm here? Knows that I had that information?

"Who emptied my computer files and how?"

"My cousin. He's a computer genius, I guess you could say. He told me some other things about you too."

I try to keep my face void of emotion. "Like what?"

"Like that your mother died when you were three in a single car accident and that you were found a few days later. That you grew up in foster care, and that your last address was the juvenile detention center in Blackwood, New Jersey."

My heart rate picks up and blood drums against my ears.

"How did he...?"

"We'll talk about all that later, but I want to know something else first."

"What?"

"Joshua Blake. I assume he's the Josh you named *my* son after. The one you called out for when we were together last."

I feel the blood drain from my face.

He shifts his attention to the vodka, refreshes his glass, then pushes it toward me.

"You look like you may need this, Kat."

"It's Katie," I say absently. "I'm Katie now."

He shakes his head. "Not for much longer, sweetheart. Drink that."

I look down at the clear liquid, set my mug aside, and drink the contents of his glass. He's right. I need it.

"Your cousin...does he know where we are?"

"He's not a danger to you."

"But we are in danger? Josh and me?"

It's his turn to swallow the freshly poured vodka in his glass. "I won't let anything happen to either of you. Now tell me why my son is named after another man."

I tilt my head to the side because is he for real? "Did you really think I'd name him after you? After what I saw?" I feel my eyebrows creep up my forehead.

"Not so much that, although it would have been

nice, but specifically that you named him after another boyfriend."

"Joshua wasn't a boyfriend. He was my foster brother and my friend. I told you that already a long time ago. Lev, you ki—" I stop, lower my voice, and glance toward the doorway. Josh sometimes comes out for a glass of water. It's usually when he's scared. "After what happened, do you think I wanted to have anything to do with you?"

"I told you, I didn't hurt Nina. She wasn't supposed to die."

"Whether you did or didn't, back then, I know what I saw."

"I want to know about Joshua Blake."

"We were in the same foster home together at one point. Joshua, Cassie, and me. That's all."

"Who's Cassie?"

"Joshua's younger sister. She was thirteen, I was fifteen, and Joshua was sixteen." I push my chair back and stand. "And I don't want to talk about this."

He catches my wrist. "Sit."

"I mean it, Lev. I don't want to talk about it."

He squeezes my wrist, and I'm reminded again how much bigger than me he is. How much stronger. "I said sit."

I do.

"How did Joshua die?"

I shift my gaze away.

"How did you end up in juvie?"

I wrap my hands around my lukewarm mug of tea.

"Why were your records sealed?"

I turn to him. "Why don't you ask your cousin?" I say, standing and slipping out of reach before he can grab me again. "I'm going to bed."

18

LEV

I'm half tempted to crawl into bed and bury myself inside Kat again, but unfortunately, I have more pressing matters to deal with. Vasily has been blowing my goddamn phone up all day, and I can't put him off any longer.

Once I hear the springs creak in Kat's mattress, I step outside into the dark of night and wander just far enough out of earshot. I wouldn't put it past Kat to sneak around and listen to my conversations at this point, dissecting every word for any excuse she might need to run again. I'm not prepared to let that happen, and I know we still have a lot of shit to figure out. But Vasily's patience is running out, and so is my time here.

"Levka." Vasily growls into the phone on the second ring. "What the fuck is going on?"

"I've been chasing a lead." My breath billows into the brisk Colorado air. "I told you that."

"You've ignored my texts. My phone calls." His rage is palpable through the phone. I don't have to see him to know the vein in his forehead is pulsating. "I want my fucking answers, and I want them now!"

Something shatters in the background, and I cringe as his voice pierces through my eardrum. Vasily is losing his fucking mind over this. It doesn't matter what I say to assure him that Kat isn't a threat, he's been dead set that he won't rest until she's gone.

"Where the fuck is she?" he snarls at me. "I want a location, Lev. And I want her goddamn head on a platter. Do you understand?"

My blood heats, and I grind down my jaw to keep myself from saying something stupid. I owe my uncle a great deal. He raised me. Fed me. Taught me everything he knows. He is blood, but Kat and Josh are my family. I realize it when I glance at the cabin and think of them sleeping soundly inside. Depending on me to protect them.

"I'm putting Andrei on a plane tomorrow," Vasily barks. "I want a fucking address. Tell me where you are."

"That isn't necessary." I pinch the bridge of my nose to stem the headache starting to take root. "I'm on my way back. I'll explain everything when I get there. Three days. Just give me three days, Uncle."

There is a pause on the other line, and I don't know if he's going to accept my assurances anymore. He's grown suspicious of me, and I don't blame him. I've been lying to him all week, and he doesn't trust me the way he used to.

"Seventy-two hours," Vasily seethes. "Not a fucking minute more. Don't disappoint me, Lev."

With that impassioned speech, he ends the call abruptly, and I glare down at the screen. Right now, the whole fucking world is pissed off at me, and I have three goddamn days to fix it.

I walk back to the cabin and collapse into the chair on the front porch. For fourteen years, I've been doing this shit. Running jobs for Vasily. Taking every order he shoves down my throat. And what the fuck do I have to show for it? Not a goddamn thing.

I've been lying to myself, dreaming that I could ever get out. I could do things differently. But that window only grows smaller every day. And now, it's suffocating me to death.

I consider Kat and Josh. What's best for them? It sure as fuck isn't going back to Philly so she can hide out in my house while I go out and take care of business. I don't want that life for them. I don't want that life for any of us. And it occurs to me with such fucking clarity at that moment, we could do things differently. This phone in my hand—this fucking tether to Vasily—could be dropped in the nearest lake. I could pack up my family and leave here tomorrow. We could go any-fucking-where.

But even as I tell myself that, I know it's not that easy. Vasily would hunt me like a dog until he takes his last breath. Nobody betrays him, and nobody leaves this business alive.

With a sigh, I retrieve the files on my phone and thumb through them again. Alexei has sent me everything he has on Kat. Names and addresses of anyone she might be associated with, including the foster kids she knew. But chunks of her past are still missing. Chunks she is resistant to divulge. I know Mr. George died from knife wounds, and it was determined that Joshua was the assailant, but I suspect there is much more to it than that. She feels indebted to Joshua, and her affinity for knives as a source of protection are only further proof of my suspicions. But I need to hear it from Kat. She doesn't get that I'm not asking her to hurt her. It's the only way I can fully protect her.

As I'm considering all the ways my life is currently imploding, my phone rings, and I'm surprised to see it's Alexei calling. Particularly because it's much later in Massachusetts. He wouldn't be calling at this hour if it wasn't urgent.

"Lyoshenka." I pull up the screen and meet his gaze. "Is everything alright?"

"Yes." He nods. "Everything is fine here. But I have some more information I thought you might want."

"What is it?" I ask.

"Our mutual friend called me this evening. Misha tells me that Vasily has been sniffing around, asking several Vory members to assist him with some research. The name he delivered was, of course, Katerina Blake."

"Christ." My stomach churns with this new revelation. I knew Vasily was growing suspicious, but I didn't know he was going behind my back to do his own queries into the matter.

"Do you know if he's managed to find anything?" I ask.

"No." Alexei shrugs. "Unfortunately, I don't. However, Misha also told me that there were some whispers Vasily is not certain he can trust you anymore. For this reason, I thought it wise to advise you to be very careful, Levka. What you do from here on out could very well determine your fate."

"I'm aware." I lean back into the chair and consider the alternate plan that's been brewing in my mind for some time now. It was always going to be my last resort. A plan not just for a rainy day, but a fucking hurricane. Betraying my uncle is something I wouldn't have even considered two months ago, but everything changed the day I saw Kat with my son.

"Do you still have the contents of the drive?" I ask Alexei.

He nods. "For now, yes."

"Don't dispose of it just yet," I inform him. "I need that for insurance. And it's something I may require your help with."

Alexei frowns. "You know I am loyal to my Vory brothers. You are my cousin, and you have my trust, but I must know the reasons, Levka. You cannot expect me to betray our traditions—"

"I have a son," I cut him off, and my words produce an immediate understanding reflected back at me in Alexei's eyes. He may be a Vor, but first and foremost, he is a father and a husband. If there is anyone who understands the values of family, it is him.

"You have a son?" he repeats.

"With Kat," I tell him. "I didn't know, but now I do. He's three years old, and he's ours."

Alexei nods gravely and does not need further consideration than that. "Then I will do what I can to help you."

"Thank you, Lyoshenka."

I'm prepared to end the call, but before I do, he holds up his hand. "There is something else. I considered waiting until you were home to inform you, but given the information you just provided, I feel it best to inform you now."

"What is it?"

He pauses, his eyes pinching with uncharacteristic emotion. Alexei rarely shows his emotions in such a way, and it gives me pause.

"Lyoshenka?"

"One of the names on your hard drive," he says solemnly. "Roger Benson. He was a neighbor in your mother's apartment building. Did you realize that?"

"No." I rub at my temples. "I didn't."

"I thought it seemed out of place myself," Alexei adds. "He was not a cop or a politician or anyone of importance, yet he was on the list. Oddly enough, he was killed exactly one week after your mother's death."

Ice fills my lungs as I consider the implication. "Did he see something?"

"Officially, no," Alexei answers. "But unofficially, he filed a police report with an Officer Stanton, who, in case you hadn't noticed, was another name on that drive. Stanton was also killed within the week, and whatever the report may have contained, it disappeared."

He doesn't have to say anything else. The implications of his statement weigh heavy on my soul. That hard drive was stolen from Vasily. A drive he's been more insistent about than anything else he's ever asked of me because it could ruin him. Words straight from his own mouth. It doesn't take a logician to connect the dots, but I don't want to accept what I have always suspected deep down.

"I'm still digging," Alexei tells me.

"I need something concrete..." I choke out. "I need to see the proof with my own eyes."

He nods as if to say he understands, but his words contradict that. "I will do my best. But sometimes, I think you know, the truth is best found in our guts."

19

KAT

It takes me a full minute to register that the sun is creeping brightly around the curtains of my bedroom, and I'm still in bed. I blink my eyes several times, rolling to my side and away from the sunlight that woke me. I hug the pillow as my mind works, as I register the distinctly masculine scent on the bed.

I bolt upright the moment I remember.

Lev.

He crept into my bed late. I woke up for all of a second when he did, but I remember him gathering me into his arms and then nothing else. I slept. I slept better than I have in a long time.

The bedroom door is closed, but I hear the sound of the TV. One of Josh's cartoons is on. I throw the blankets off and hurry out of bed, panic gripping me as that thought is back.

What if he takes Josh? What if he leaves with Josh?

My heart is racing as I reach the door, but when I open it, I hear them. Lev is saying something, and I think he's trying to keep his voice quiet, but it's so deep it's almost a rumble when he whispers.

Josh giggles. Tells him the marshmallows are the best part.

"Hey, you're taking them all," Lev says.

"Shh. Don't tell Mommy."

I walk into the kitchen. "Don't tell Mommy what?" I ask as I see Josh standing on his chair arm deep inside the box of cereal, his bowl already stacked with marshmallows and a few pieces of cereal, which probably got there accidentally.

"Busted," Lev says, and I notice he, too, has a pile of marshmallows in his bowl.

"Mommy!" Josh wraps his arms around my neck when I get to him. I lift him out of his seat. He's already dressed in a pair of jeans and a sweater.

"You're up early," I tell him, brushing his hair back with my fingers.

"Lev helped me," he says.

When I release him, he sits back down and attempts to pick up the carton of milk.

"Let me get that," Lev says, taking it from Josh's

hands and pouring milk over the bowl of little colorful marshmallows.

Josh picks up his spoon, and we both watch him for a minute as he spoons the cereal and brings it to his mouth, holding his other hand underneath to catch the dripping milk.

I look at Lev's face, and he's smiling like he's in awe. Like he's the proudest father in the world.

He shifts his gaze up to mine, and I school my features, hardening my expression as I turn to pour myself a cup of the coffee he's already made.

I become aware then that I'm still in my nightie. I don't have a clue what my hair looks like, and I haven't brushed my teeth yet. I know I shouldn't care, hell, I should be happy if I repel him, but he comes over to me and lays a possessive hand on my hip.

"Morning," he says, looking me over, brushing hair back from my face. He leans toward me and kisses my cheek. That brushing of his lips and the tickle of the scruff against my face send a tremor through me, and I remember what happened yesterday, what we did on my bedroom floor.

As if he, too, is remembering, he slides his hand down to cup my ass and squeezes.

I wince, remembering that too, and shove his arm away.

He grins, eyes gleaming. I can almost see the

dirty thoughts going through his head as he grabs my ass again. "Still hurt?" he asks. Then he leans in and says more quietly, "I'll have a look in a minute. Rub the tender spots."

I push him away again and give him a glare. I walk to my son and put my hands on his shoulders. "Why didn't you wake me up this morning?" Josh usually wakes me up at the crack of dawn on the weekends. I swear that kid can sleep in every weekday when he has to get up for school, but come the weekend, he's up before the sun.

He shrugs a shoulder. "Lev said you were tired."

"Did he?" I glance up at Lev to find his expression serious as he types something into his phone.

"We're going on a plane, Mommy!" Josh cries out before shoving another spoonful of what is essentially sugar into his mouth.

"What are you talking about, silly?"

Lev's dark eyes flash toward me, but a ding from his phone snares his attention again.

"Lev's taking us on a trip."

Lev puts his phone to his ear and walks into the other room. Again, he's trying to keep his voice down, but I can't understand what he's saying anyway. He's speaking in Russian.

"Done!" Josh announces and bounds off the chair as the opening song of one of his favorite cartoons comes on.

Leaving my coffee where it is, I follow Lev's voice, which is coming from my bedroom. When I get there, I find him standing over my open purse, holding what I think is my driver's license. My wallet lies on the bed beside the purse.

I see the flash of the camera, and a moment later, he tucks his phone into his back pocket.

"What are you doing?" I ask, taking my license from his hand and putting it back into my wallet.

"I needed your photo."

"For what?"

"A new ID." He checks the time on the clock beside the bed. "We should get going. Pack some things, just essentials."

"What are you talking about? I'm not going anywhere, and neither is Josh, and you can't tell him you're taking him on a plane."

He tilts his head to the side to study me, and I decide I hate that look. It's the one that says you'll do as you're told without using any words at all.

Lev walks around me, closes and locks the door, then returns to take my arms. He gives the tiniest squeeze. I don't miss its meaning.

"I'm going to say that again, Katerina. I need you to pack some things, just essentials. I already gathered Josh's birth certificate and all your papers. When you're finished with your things, pack what

Josh needs. We can buy anything you forget later, but we leave within the hour."

I shove his arms off. "I'm going to say this again, Lev," I try for the same tone he just used with me. "I'm not going anywhere, and neither is Josh. You, however, are free to leave whenever you want."

He grins like he's humoring me. There's that tilt of the head again. I want to tell him to go fuck himself, but I remember how that turned out the last time.

Lev steps closer, and I'd back up, but the bed is behind me, so I end up dropping into a seat. His grin widens, and he leans down, hands on either side of me on the bed so I have to lean uncomfortably backward.

His eyes roam my face, then down to where the nightie lies open against my chest, down over my belly to my bare thighs.

I look down too, see how high it's ridden and swallow hard when his eyes, now darker, shift back to mine.

My heart races because I recognize that look, and it's the one that makes my belly flutter.

Lev leans closer, makes a point of inhaling.

"I smell you," he says in a whisper, the fingers of one hand brushing my inner thigh.

I make a sound as he leans closer, forcing me backward as his fingers rise higher and higher.

"And I bet you're wet."

He does that thing again where he brushes that scruff along my cheek, and I swallow, my legs opening of their own accord as his fingers come just inches from my core.

With his other hand, he pushes me to lie all the way back and straightens. I follow his gaze as he lifts my nightie up to my belly, his eyes on my exposed sex.

I hadn't worn panties last night because it hurt, so I try to get up to cover myself.

"No, don't," he says, pushing my hand away. "Don't hide yourself from me. This pussy belongs to me, Katerina." He brushes his fingers through the neat triangle of hair. "I like this little bit of pretty red hair." He crouches down.

"Lev—"

"*You* belong to me."

"I don't—"

"And I like seeing how wet you are for me." He pushes my legs wider as he leans his face close, so close I gasp in anticipation of his mouth on me, ready for it, wanting it. But he just inhales and meets my eyes with a wide grin. "You want my mouth on you, don't you?"

I fist the blankets, wanting to want to kick him away, to kick him in the face, but he's right, and he knows it.

"You want me to make you come?"

"Josh is—"

"Door's locked, and Josh is busy." He closes his mouth over me then, and I cover my mouth to muffle my gasp when he circles my clit with his tongue before pulling back, standing, undoing his jeans and fisting his thick cock. "Open your legs."

I do, licking my lips and hating myself a little as I spread my legs for him, but it's not wide enough because he puts his hands on my thighs and forces them wider, and as his eyes never leave mine, he thrusts into me.

I squeeze my hand over my mouth, and he grins, replacing it with one of his as he fucks me hard and fast.

The bed creaks beneath us as I stretch for him and he pushes my nightie up to expose my breasts. He dips his head down and takes a nipple into his mouth, and when I cry out, he presses his hand harder to my mouth, teeth tugging at my nipple. I'm so close, one more thrust, and fuck, I'm coming.

I close my eyes and arch my back, and I come, and I feel him thicken inside me. He lays his weight on me, face inches from mine, hands on either side of my head, making me look at him. He watches me, and I watch him as we come together, and I think he's so beautiful. So fucking beautiful like this.

"You're mine, Kat. Mine."

He kisses me with his final thrusts, and I swallow his moan and dig my fingernails into his back as he finally stills, muscles tight, body rigid, all his weight on me making it hard to breathe.

When he draws back, we're both breathless, and I see the sheen of sweat on his forehead as he smiles down at me.

"Fuck, Kat. You make me crazy, you know that?"

He pulls out, but when I move to get up, he doesn't let me. Instead, he cups his hand at my open legs, and I'm still so sensitive I gasp.

"Shh," he tells me.

"Let me up." I need to clean up. I feel the cum sliding out of me.

"Where were we?" he asks, rubbing cum all over me, over my pussy and my clit, building tension again. "Kat?"

"I hate you," I groan.

"No, that's not it. I was telling you that you belong to me." He grins wide. "And you wish you hated me." He winks, then pulls his hand away when I'm seconds from coming again, and I groan. He flips me slightly to my side and slaps my hip. "Now get up, get cleaned up, and go pack Josh's and your things. One duffel." He points at the bag he's conveniently taken out of my closet for me.

His phone rings, and he wipes his wet fingers across my belly, adjusts his jeans, and answers in Russian, gesturing for me to get moving.

20

KAT

"Can you at least tell me where we're going?" I ask as he closes the door after buckling a very excited Josh into the back of the Jeep. "Or for how long? I have a job, you know."

He's serious again as he opens the passenger door for me to get in.

"Philly," he says.

I feel myself pale. Back to Philly? But that's where all the trouble is. "Why? Why would you take us back there?"

"Get in."

He lifts me in when I don't move right away and pulls the strap across my chest, clicking it into place. His expression is serious, not at all like the first time I got into his car, the sporty Audi I was so impressed with, and he strapped me in and I waited for him to kiss me.

"Do you think you're safe here? Do you think Vasily's influence doesn't stretch this far?"

The coffee turns to acid in my belly.

His face softens as he must see how scared I am, because it's as if I only realize at that moment that it's not Lev I have to be afraid of. At least it's not only Lev. It's the rest of them too.

Josh's voice registers in my hearing. He's singing the tune of the cartoon he was just watching, and I think I'm going to be sick.

"Hey." Lev brushes hair back behind my ear. "I told you I'm not going to let anyone hurt you or Josh. I'll kill anyone who tries."

I look into his dark eyes, and what I see there is not what I expect. Tenderness, genuine tenderness, but there's an edge to it. Because I know he means what he's saying. I know he will kill anyone who tries. I know well what he's capable of.

And I think that's the hardest part.

"Mommy?"

Lev lifts his gaze to Josh over my shoulder, and I study him for a moment longer, that hard line of his jaw, the set of his mouth. His big, powerful hands resting on my thighs.

And even though I trust that the tenderness I just saw was genuine, I know that if I can, if I get even the smallest opportunity, I need to get Josh and myself away from him.

"Yes, baby?" I say, turning to Josh.

"Did you get Wally?" Wally is the stuffed bear he's had since he was born.

"Yes, sweetheart." I reach into my purse and pull the well-loved bear out and notice my passport is in there, too. "Here he is." I hand Wally to Josh.

Lev closes the door and comes around to the driver's seat. He starts the engine, and when we drive away, I glance back at the little house and think about how much I liked it. Liked being here. Because I don't know if I'll ever see it again. If we'll ever be back.

A text alert has Lev reaching into his pocket as he takes the turn out of town and heads toward the highway. He reads it but doesn't reply and tucks the phone back into his pocket.

"What time is our flight?" I ask.

"Late afternoon. We have to tie up some loose ends."

"What loose ends?"

He glances in the rearview mirror. Josh is busy showing Wally the sights.

"Don't worry about it. I'll take care of everything," he says.

It's a long, tense two hours to Denver as Lev takes

calls while driving. He speaks in Russian, so I can't understand a word he's saying.

Just outside of Denver, he pulls into the parking lot of a Marriott.

"Stay here," he says, parking beside a large, black SUV. He takes the keys of the Jeep and meets my gaze across the front seat. "Don't be stupid."

A warning.

He closes and locks the doors.

Josh has nodded off, and I watch as Lev transfers our duffel and another one into the back of the SUV, then walks into the front entrance of the hotel. It's barely two minutes before he's back, but instead of getting into the driver's seat again, he opens my door.

"Get out."

My heart drops into my belly. I glance back at a sleeping Josh.

"What?"

"Out, Kat." He undoes my belt and closes his hand over my arm.

I slip out of the Jeep, and he closes the door, walks me to the back, leaves me there as he opens the back door and lifts Josh's seat out. When the hell did he figure out how to do that? Just yesterday, he didn't know how the straps worked.

"What are you doing?" I start, panic gripping hold of me as I take the other side of Josh's seat.

"Mommy?" Josh asks, waking up, rubbing his eyes.

"Shh," Lev says, smiling down at him. "We're almost there. You're going to ride in my car now."

"What?" I'm white-knuckling Josh's child seat.

"Help me strap his seat in, Kat," Lev says, warning me with his eyes. He opens the back door to the SUV. It smells brand new.

"Lev?" I start, but he ignores me, puts the seat into the back seat, and places his body between me and Josh as he secures the child seat to the car.

"Wow," Josh says. "This is nice."

"Wait until you get on the airplane, kiddo," Lev says.

Lev turns and closes the door, then walks me the few steps backward to the Jeep.

"You're not taking him. You can't take him!"

He takes my right wrist, turns my hand palm up, and drops my keys in them. At that moment, I realize how powerless I am. How stupid. If he wants Josh, I've just made it that much easier for him to kidnap my son.

I look up to find his dark eyes on me.

He wouldn't take my son, would he? Is this my punishment for running away when I was pregnant with his baby? Does he still blame me for that?

"Please don't take my son from me." Tears burn my eyes.

"Katya." He cups my face, wiping the tears from my cheeks, and something about the way he says my name tugs at my heart. "Josh is my family."

I feel my knees buckle, and it takes all I have to keep upright. "You can't. Please—"

"*You're* my family." He pulls me to him and puts his lips to my forehead. He holds me there for a long minute, and I feel myself go soft. When he draws back, I look up at him. "Do you think I would take our son away from his mother? Didn't you hear me when I told you that you belong to me? I take care of what's mine, Katya. You and the boy are mine. Now get yourself together. Your passport is in your bag. You need to check in for your flight to Florida."

"Florida? You said...you said..." I'm hyperventilating. I try to push him away and go to Josh.

"Look at me," he says, taking my arms and giving me a little shake. "Get yourself together and look at me."

I look up at him.

"You need to drive to the airport and park your car. Leave the keys inside and check in for your flight to Florida. I've sent you the ticket on your phone. Once you check in, you'll bypass security and walk to Terminal B. You'll exit the airport there. Josh and I will be waiting for you, and from there, we'll get to our real flight to Philly. This way, if anyone is looking for you, they'll think you've gone to Florida."

"But—"

"We're pressed for time now." He reaches into his back pocket and takes out an envelope. From inside it, he hands me a new phone. "After you check in, take the SIM card out of your old phone and flush it, then throw your phone away. You'll call me with this once you're on your way to Terminal B, and I'll come get you. Understand?"

"I want to take Josh with me."

He shakes his head. "Can't do that. I have your new passport, and I'll hold on to his until you meet us."

There's a knock on the window, and I see Josh's bright face as he waves to us.

"Pull yourself together for him. You don't want him upset."

"Can I at least kiss him and explain what's happening?" I ask, turning away from the window and wiping the last of my tears.

Lev nods, tucks my hair behind my ears, and opens the back door.

"It's a nice car, Mommy. We should get one like this."

I try to smile, but it falters. "Let's get to Philly first. Lev's going to drive you to the airport, okay? I have to drop off the Jeep, but I'll see you there, okay? I'll see you at the airport, and we'll get on the airplane together, okay?"

"Okay, Mommy."

I lean in to kiss him. "I love you, baby," I say, hugging him as best I can while he's still strapped into his seat.

"I love you, Mommy."

21

LEV

Kat's voice is tense when I answer her call, and it's clear she's still uncertain whether I'll actually be waiting for her outside.

"I'm on my way," she says. "Just about to walk through the doors."

"We're pulling up to the curb now," I assure her. "We'll be right outside."

She's quiet but doesn't hang up, and when she finally walks through the doors and spots us waiting for her, the tension melts from her body. She hurries over to the SUV and climbs inside, glancing back at Josh.

"Hey, buddy, are you okay?"

"Yeah, Mommy." He gives her a sleepy nod.

She glances at me too, and I squeeze her thigh

beneath my palm before steering us back out into traffic. "It's called trust, Kat. We'll get there."

"Where are we going now?" She stares out the window as I drive.

"Now we're going to another airport."

She nods as if she's numb to the fact that I've uprooted her life like this. A small part of me feels guilty for that, but if keeping her safe causes her some discomfort, I'll deal with that any day of the week so long as she's still alive.

"You were right, you know." Her wavering voice distracts me from the road, and when I look over at her, I can't identify the source of concern on her face.

"Right about what?" I reach over and turn her face toward me. "What is it?"

Her lip trembles, and her eyes are glassy as she shakes her head. She peeks over her shoulder to make sure Josh isn't listening before she speaks.

"One of the teachers from school called me on my way to the airport," she tells me. "She said two men showed up there today, Lev. They were looking for me, and they spoke another language. She thought maybe Russian."

Acid fills my gut as I process her words. This is the manifestation of my worst fears. Vasily doesn't trust me anymore, and now he's coming after her himself. But what's even worse is the fact that he tracked her down here. Something that took me four years to do myself. The question is how.

"They were in my classroom," Kat continues. "Nobody knows how they'd even got into the building since it wasn't a school day. The teachers had meetings all day. So, it must be them, right? It must be Vasily's men?"

"Probably." I squeeze her thigh again, opting for a neutral tone. She doesn't need to doubt my abilities to keep her safe. That's the last thing I want. "But it's going to be okay. You're with me now."

"I just keep thinking about it." She shakes her head, silent tears splashing against her cheeks. "What if we were there, Lev? What would they have done to us?"

"You weren't there." My fingers tighten on the steering wheel. "And they aren't going to do anything to you. I will keep you safe, sweetheart. Even if it's the last thing I ever do."

My ominous words don't seem to bring her any comfort. Kat curls into herself, wiping away her tears and distracting herself with the passing scenery.

"I just can't believe this is my life," she murmurs, so quietly I almost don't hear her.

I know what she means. If she hadn't gotten mixed up with me, this wouldn't be happening right now. And a part of me wishes she hadn't. But yet another part of me selfishly doesn't give a fuck.

Because she's mine now, and regardless of the impending storm ahead, I intend to keep it that way.

"Everything will be okay. You'll see."

We fall into a tense silence while I navigate the two-hour drive to Cheyenne. Josh does surprisingly well for the duration of the trip, napping for most of it. Kat starts to doze off but wakes up just as we cross the border into Wyoming, and her nerves return when I eventually park the SUV at Sloan Airport.

"This is a small airport," she observes. "Are we actually flying out of here?"

"Yes." I shoot off a quick text to Alexei and receive confirmation within a minute. When I get out to grab the bags, it isn't long before Kostya appears to greet us.

"Levka." He holds out his hand in offer, and I shake it. "It is nice to meet you in person. Lyoshenka has told me many stories over the years."

"Good, I hope?" I grin at him.

"Eh." His lips tilt up at the corners. "They can't all be good in this big family of ours, can they? Now, let me help you with your bags. I'll show your family to the plane."

I thank him and offload the bags before walking around to meet Kat as she's taking Josh's seat out of the car.

"I can carry him," she says as I hoist him up into my arms.

"I know you can." I swat her on the ass. "But so can I."

She narrows her eyes at me, and Kostya interjects, insisting on carrying the car seat as well. After I lock the SUV, he leads us out onto the secure airstrip and to our waiting plane.

Kat's eyes widen, and she jerks her neck up to look at me.

"Is that for us?"

"The plane!" Josh squeals. "We're going on a plane!"

"That would be the one."

"A private jet?" she frowns. "How is this even possible?"

"I had to call in a few favors," I admit. And dump a lot of cash, but she doesn't need to know that part. Lucky for me, Alexei is well connected.

"Hello, Lev." Pavel, the pilot, greets us from the stairway.

"Afternoon, Pavel. Thank you for flying us today."

"It is no problem." He shakes his head. "Whatever Lyoshenka asks, I will do. I owe him a great deal."

I nod, and he gestures for us to board.

"Come, let's get your family settled in, yes?"

He helps Kat up the stairs, and I follow with Josh. The benefits of a private jet are no security lines and a much quicker process than commercial. Within minutes, we are loaded onto the plane and secured for takeoff.

Josh squeals with excitement as the engine rumbles to life. Despite Kat's nerves, I catch her smiling more than a few times as she watches our son experience his first flight. It's an occasion I wish was under better circumstances.

The reality is, once we get to Philly, everything will change. There will be no more carefree moments like this. Not until I have executed my exit strategy with Alexei's help. This could take time, and still involve many risks. Vasily is always temperamental, but lately, he has been a loose cannon. Keeping Kat and Josh safe while appeasing him will be the biggest challenge I've ever faced. But as I study their faces, committing them to memory at this moment just as they are, I know it will be worth every bit of pain I may endure.

WE TOUCH down in Baltimore just after midnight. Josh is fast asleep, exhausted from our big adventure of the day, and Kat looks well on her way too. But she is nervous as I load them into the waiting SUV that Alexei organized for us. She seems aware of my own tension as we hit the freeway and make the two-hour drive back to Philly.

Eventually, she falls back asleep, and I attempt to organize the thoughts running through my mind. For the past few days, I've managed to forget what coming back here would entail. But it is not so easy now. And when I finally pull up to the safe house just after two a.m., it feels like I've been punched in the gut as I consider what happens next. I have difficulty trusting others, but in this instance, I will have no choice.

Kat is still fast asleep beside me, unaware that I'm watching her. Studying the lines of her face, the fall of her hair. At that moment, the thought that I could ever lose her hits me like a punch to the gut. I want more than to simply call her mine. I want her to be my wife and take my last name and make me more beautiful children. I want all of those things with her.

But for right now, tonight is all we have. And I try not to let that sour my mood as I stir her from sleep with a kiss.

"Are we here?" She blinks and sits upright, glancing at the unfamiliar house in confusion. "What is this place?"

"It's a safe house," I tell her. "Come on."

She doesn't seem convinced that it's actually safe, but when I get out and start unbuckling Josh, she is quick to follow. I carry him to the door, and Kat glances up at me nervously as I knock. When Pasha answers, he gestures us inside, but Kat is frozen to the doorstep.

"Who is this?" she asks.

"It's a friend," I assure her. More specifically, he is one of Alexei's latest recruits. Still somewhat green, but highly trustworthy, and right now, he's the only available option I have.

Kat doesn't seem to warm to the idea of him hanging around, even as we enter the house and get settled in. I show her around the place, which consists of the basics. There are two bedrooms and a bathroom. Not a lot of furniture, but enough to stay here for a while at least. I also note that Alexei had the second room done up with a child-sized bed and plenty of books and toys. Probably something his wife encouraged, but regardless, I am grateful.

"Will he be okay in here?" Kat asks nervously as I lay Josh into the bed.

"Yes." I point at the window, which has been sealed shut. "That glass? It's bulletproof, Kat. And this monitor will let you see anything that goes on in this room from any part of the house. There is also a keypad on every door, which I will give you the code for."

She swallows and glances down at our son, her

eyes glassy and her face fraught with emotion. "Okay. As long as I can see him."

After giving Josh a kiss, we exit the room and join Pasha in the living room. It's late, and we're all tired, but I don't have a lot of time. Tomorrow morning, I will need to leave her here with him, and I need her to know that it's okay.

Pasha seems to understand my unspoken thoughts as he offers her something to drink, and then proceeds to show her that the pantry and fridge are fully stocked. When Kat declines, he makes small talk, pointing out some other features of the house and asking her conversational questions to get her talking a little.

While they do that, I grab the bags and scope out the street. It's a quiet suburban neighborhood where neighbors keep to themselves and the only prowlers to be seen are cats with bells on their collars. Alexei has done well by my family, and for that, I am eternally grateful.

Once I'm back inside, I thank Pasha for his help and take Kat to the other bedroom. She's got the monitor in her hand, constantly checking on Josh, and I can tell she won't be getting any sleep tonight in her current frame of mind.

"Is Pasha staying here too?" she asks.

"Yes." I remove her coat and slowly undress her,

helping her into her nightgown and pulling back the covers for her to climb into bed.

"Where are you going?" She frowns as I move toward the door.

"I'll be right back."

When I return a few moments later, with Josh cradled in my arms, she looks relieved as I lay him beside her.

"Just for tonight," I tell her. "Until you feel comfortable here."

Kat kisses his forehead and watches as I remove my shoes and coat, and then lay down on the outside of the bed, still in my shirt and jeans.

"Do you think this is a good idea?" She worries her lip between her teeth. "If he wakes up and sees us all sleeping together—"

"Then he will start to understand that we are a family." I lean over and kiss her lips. "Now go to sleep, sweetheart. Tomorrow is a new day."

22

LEV

After a long-winded talk and many assurances to Kat that she would be safe at the house with Pasha, I find myself back at Delirium, awaiting Vasily's arrival. Already, Andrei is studying me, a smirk playing across his lips like he knows something I don't. If I could, I would wipe that smirk clean from his face with a rusty knife.

"Levka." Vasily slams the door behind him as he enters the private room upstairs. The same room where I first brought Kat into my life.

"Uncle." I greet him with a nod.

He sits down across the table from me, his gaze meeting mine. Neither of us speaks as we size each other up. I know better than to be too eager with information. And now that I'm aware he's been going behind my back to find his own answers, I must maintain my poker face. A part of me still hopes he will come clean and admit it. That he will prove he isn't the man I'm beginning to think he is.

"Any word on the girl?" He shatters my hopes with a single sentence.

"I tracked her for a few weeks, but she seems to be ahead of us."

He scratches at the stubble on his chin, cocking his head to the side. "What made you believe she was in Florida?"

"She has a connection there," I say. "A friend."

He considers my statement, which he knows is a lie, but I wait for him to call me on it.

"And the drive?"

"Still nothing." I stare into the dark abyss of his eyes, wondering if my own blood could really be responsible for my mother's death. His own sister. But even as I question it, I don't doubt that he would kill Kat without a second thought. Vasily is only loyal to one thing, and that is his own selfish desires. He may be a Vor, but he won't hesitate to forsake his beloved brethren if it saves his own skin. Of that, I have no doubt.

"You have disappointed me," he says without emotion. "I expected this to be taken care of long ago. It has gone on too long, and I can't afford to spare you any longer. I need you back to work."

My jaw grinds together as I consider what he has planned. But all I can do is simply nod. It's what he expects of me. What he has always expected of me.

"What do you need me to do?" I ask.

"You can start by helping Andrei with some cleanup this afternoon."

My stomach churns as I nod. "Done."

Vasily dismisses us, and I follow Andrei out onto the street. But when he heads for his car, I shake my head.

"Let's take mine."

He hesitates for a moment before getting inside. Typically, I wouldn't want my car near anything we might be about to encounter, but right now, it's imperative I have it available at all times. On the off chance that Kat does call me with an emergency, I can dump this moron on a street corner and get to her fast.

Andrei fiddles with my stereo and tries to light up a cigarette while I start the engine, which I quickly pluck out of his hand and toss out the window.

"What the fuck?" he grumbles.

"Not in my car. Where are we going?"

"My place," he says.

Fucking great. I spend the entirety of the twenty-minute drive to his house wondering what kind of mess he's left for me this time. Whatever it is, it can't be good.

My theory is regretfully proven correct when he leads me into his bedroom, and I find a woman still handcuffed to his bedframe. Her face is beaten so badly she's unidentifiable, and there's blood spatter clear up to the ceiling. The body is already starting to smell, and it's obvious this happened some time ago.

"Fucking Christ." I turn to him with so much repressed rage, it takes all of my willpower not to cave his skull in right now. "What the fuck did you do, Andrei?"

"Things got out of control." He shrugs. "Nothing I can do about it now."

I grind my jaw and pace the length of his bedroom. Fuck this shit. Andrei is so goddamned out of control, Vasily has to see it. He has to know there's no coming back from this. Every time I turn around, he's destroying something else. Or someone else. The only logical conclusion is to put him down like a rabid dog.

It's a certainty I feel deep in my gut as I take in the scene before me. I don't know who she is, but that's irrelevant. This woman didn't deserve this. And I'm sure she has a family out there somewhere.

People who will wonder what happened to her. Now I have to make her disappear, and they will never find peace in their lives.

"How do you want to do this?" Andrei asks.

He's too fucking dumb to come up something on his own, and as usual, it's left up to me. But this time, I couldn't care less about cleaning this up properly. Bringing some heat down on Vasily can only help me. Any distraction will work in my favor until I can get my shit sorted out. It's a risk, but right now, it's one I'm willing to take.

"Go grab the bleach and some gloves," I tell him.

Andrei disappears into the kitchen, and while he's doing that, I snap a good fifteen pictures of the scene. Enough that there are identifiers of his bedroom. It's not a guarantee, but it's another insurance policy.

When he returns, I strip off my jacket and get to work. Andrei uncuffs her and rolls her up in the bedding while I hold back the urge to vomit all over his bedroom. When he's done that, I point at the gloves and the bleach and tell him to get to work. He can't clean for shit, but that's exactly why it needs to be him.

"What are you going to do with her?" he asks as I start dragging the rolled-up bedding out of his bedroom.

"We're going to plant a garden. Brighten up the place a little."

"In the backyard?" He frowns.

"She's not fucking going anywhere in my car." I glare at him. "You should have thought of that before you did this."

He doesn't say a word, and it's settled. Vasily never asks what I do with the bodies. He just asks if it's taken care of. Unless Andrei decides to open his fat trap, there's a good chance he'll never know about this sloppily executed job. At least, not until I need him to.

Once I have the body in the kitchen, I open the garage and start digging through the piles of shit Andrei has accumulated over the years. I don't know why he's even bothered to keep half of it. There are at least a dozen boxes full of junk that I have to kick out of the way to get to the shovel. And it's just my fucking luck that one of them rips at the side, scattering the contents all over the concrete floor.

For fuck's sake.

I kneel and start shoveling the contents back into the box, but as I'm doing that, something catches my eye. At first glance, I don't know why I pause. Only that it feels familiar. It isn't until I pick up the small hand-carved trinket box that it comes back to me. The etching on the top is exactly like the one that sat on my mother's nightstand. But this couldn't be hers.

Even as I tell myself that, I'm hesitant to open it up. To confirm what I never wanted to believe. Because if it was hers, this would be a betrayal of the worst kind. A betrayal I could never come back from.

The hinges creak as I lift the lid, my lungs frozen as I peer inside at what is undoubtedly my mother's jewelry. Her rings, a necklace, a bracelet. But I still don't want to believe it. I can't accept it until I pop the locket open and see a photograph of our family staring back at me.

I claw at my neck, tugging the collar of my shirt down. I feel like I can't fucking breathe. What the fuck? How did this get here? How the fuck did this get here?

The echo of Andrei's footsteps in the house snaps me out of my delirium. Slamming the lid shut, I stuff the wooden box into my pocket and leave the rest of the shit on the floor. When he opens the door to the garage, I have the shovel in my grasp and a wild look in my eye. That I can be sure of.

Andrei gives me a questioning look but seems to disregard my sour mood. "I'm done cleaning. What should I do now?"

I stare at him for a beat too long, considering how bad it would be if I tortured him right here in his garage. If I cut off every one of his goddamn appendages and stuffed them down his own throat before I jammed a knife through his skull. It's what I would have done. Two weeks ago, before Kat and Josh, I wouldn't have hesitated. But right now, things need to go smoothly. This needs to be a clean break. And I need to fucking think before I act on my impulses because right now, I just want to beat him until his blood explodes across the ceiling.

"Go to the store and get some plants." I toss him my car keys. "Whatever the fuck you can find this time of year."

He nods and heads back for the house. But before he does, I stop him.

"Who was she?" I ask. "The woman in your bed?"

"Just some slut from the club," he says, confirming my suspicions. While it's likely that Vasily has already deleted the video of that night, there is a strong possibility there is other surveillance from the street. Something I'm counting on.

"Don't take too long," I tell him. "And don't get any fucking blood in my car."

He stumbles out the door and leaves me to my thoughts. I just want to get the fuck out of here. I need to check on Kat and Josh, and I need to sort through the facts before I do anything rash. There's also still the matter of meeting with Alexei this week. The sooner I can get out of this shithole, the better.

I haul the shovel out into the backyard and use

my simmering rage as motivation. Three hours later, Andrei has a new garden. A hodgepodge of plants and flowers that will certainly be dead within the week. But for now, it's enough to satisfy the bare minimum. At least until I can figure out how to destroy this sick bastard for good.

23

KAT

Pasha spends the day trying to keep to the background, but Josh is curious and somehow manages to snare him in a game of hide-and-seek in the afternoon.

I get one text from Lev all day. It's brief, telling me he'll miss dinner and that he'll be home late.

I want to tell him this isn't home. I feel anxious and the opposite of safe even though this is supposed to be a *safe* house.

But taking Josh and leaving, I can't do that. I know that. Not that I'd be able to. I have a feeling Pasha is here to make sure we stay in as much as to keep the bad guys out. The few times I've walked to the front door, he's turned up at my side in an instant, reminding me to stay away from the windows.

I think back to our drive after landing in Baltimore. I felt Lev watching me when he thought I was asleep. Well, I was asleep, and I'm not sure what exactly woke me, but all I can recall was the intensity of how he was looking at me.

And I guess what he said more than once is hitting me.

I'm his.

We're his.

"Mommy?" Josh looks up at me from where he's sitting on the floor at my feet. I realize the cartoon has ended, and his eyes are sleepy.

"Time for bed, sweetie," I tell him, standing.

On cue, Pasha turns the corner, coming toward us to take him.

"I got him," I say.

He nods, stepping backward, and returns Josh's sleepy smile. I didn't realize Russian men were so chivalrous.

Josh lays his head on my shoulder, and I carry him upstairs. I pause when I get to the door of his temporary bedroom. I eye the key in the lock on the outside of the door. Each of the bedrooms and the bathroom in the hallway have that. It's strange.

But I don't care about that now. Right now, I'm remembering what Lev said. That Josh sleeping with us was for one night. But I bypass his room and lay him down in our bed.

Our bed.

I shake my head and tuck Josh in.

"Want a story?" I ask, lying down beside him.

He nods, puts one thumb into his mouth—something he only does when he's very tired—and wraps his other hand around a lock of my hair. He closes his eyes as I start to recite from memory *Good Night, Gorilla* and can't help the tear that slides down over the bridge of my nose as I watch him sleep.

They wouldn't hurt him, would they? Would they hurt a little boy?

I was three when I lost my mom. Will history repeat for Josh? Is alive better than dead if it means foster care and caregivers like the George family?

No. Alive is always better than dead.

I slip my hair out of his hand and climb out of the bed, wiping the stray tears. From our duffel which I'd laid on a chair when we arrived, I find my scarf. I dig it out and inhale the smoke smell that still clings to it.

I go to the bathroom and lock the door. Filling the sink with warm water, I set about cleaning the scarf, draining the dirty water several times until it finally runs clear.

I think about Nina as I wash her blood away. And I think about Joshua, about when he gave me the scarf, as I squeeze the excess water out of it. He'd stolen it. We were at the mall with the Georges, and

I'd been looking at it. Mrs. George thought the pink ugly and childish and told me to leave it. I think I may have liked it even more because she hated it.

Later that night, when we were supposed to be asleep, Joshua snuck into my room and gave it to me. I still remember how surprised I'd been. How happy. I don't think I'd ever hugged anyone as hard as I hugged him that night. Over a simple scarf. It just felt like so much more at that moment. It felt good to know that someone cared about me.

When I open the bathroom door, I stop dead, my heart in my throat to find someone lurking at the bedroom entrance. I almost scream but recognize it's Lev when he moves into the little bit of light coming in from the streetlamp.

Lev puts his finger to his lips and gestures for me to follow him into the hallway.

I go, and he pulls the bedroom door closed behind us.

"I told you one night," he says. "He should sleep in his room."

His hair's wet, and he smells soapy. "That's not his room. This isn't his house. Did you just shower?"

He takes my arm, walks me into the second bedroom, and closes the door. The only light here is that from the moon coming through the split between the curtain panels.

"Where did you shower?" I ask.

"At the club."

"You went to Delirium? Why?"

"Because I have to play nice with Vasily until I get things sorted."

"Is that smart? Or safe?"

He studies me, considering, and it's that moment he takes before he answers me that makes me anxious. "It's fine. What are you doing with that?"

I look down. "Oh. I was washing it." I look around, then go to the radiator and stretch the scarf out over it to let it dry.

When I turn back to him, he's still watching me, and there's something both intense and distracted in his eyes. It's unnerving.

"What is it? Did something happen?"

He runs his hand through his still wet hair and comes to me. He takes my hand and walks backward to the bed. There, he cups the back of my head and kisses me. It's a gentle kiss, not hurried, not even erotic or at least not frantic with need.

I kiss him back, liking this, liking the warmth of him, the taste of him, the safety of him. I press myself against him and let him hold me. I like his arms around me. I think he can keep us safe. Maybe it's stupid—one man against the Russian mob—but I think he means what he said. That he'll kill anyone who tries to hurt Josh or me.

Or die trying.

A chill seeps into my veins, and I shudder.

"Shh."

I guess I'm crying again because he's holding me to him, not kissing me anymore, but his hands are moving, and he's stripping off my clothes. He's slow, patient, and methodical, and soon, I'm standing naked. He takes my hands and steps backward.

He's still fully clothed, and when I try to move to strip him, he shakes his head.

"I want to look at you now," he says.

Instinctively, I want to pull away, to hide myself, but he won't let me go. Instead, keeping hold of one hand, he reaches to switch on the lamp beside the bed.

"Lev—"

"Quiet." He has both of my hands again, and this time, he holds me at arm's length and sits on the edge of the low bed.

I feel exposed. This is different than the other times I've been naked with him. This is him looking at me, and it's somehow more intimate than when he's inside me.

"Look at me."

I don't. I can't.

"Look at me, Katya."

Katya. I like when he calls me that. He's tender when he calls me that.

I look at him, feeling my face flush. He must see

it too because he smiles a little and there's that dimple. I like when he smiles.

But then he shifts his hand up to my forearm and, with eyes still on mine, he feels the bumpy, burned skin with his thumb.

"Tell me about this."

Fuck.

I swallow, trying to contain the emotion that I force down every time I remember what happened. Remember anything that went on in that house. I keep those memories secured in boxes. It's where I like them. Where I can keep an eye on them but keep them safely locked away.

"Tell me, Katya."

A tear slides down my cheek. He doesn't move to wipe it away and won't let go of me so I can do it either.

"It was to punish Joshua, I think. And me, I guess, but more him."

More tears and Lev doesn't move. His expression doesn't change.

"I think Mr. George hated him the most. He always made him watch."

Lev's thumb stops moving, and his hands tighten on me.

"I don't think he cared one way or another about me. I could have been anyone." I pause, remembering. "Mrs. George did this. Joshua only heard it happening. Mr. George was bigger than him. He'd tie Josh up, restrain him somehow, and force him to watch. He wasn't home when she did this, and she wasn't strong enough to make Joshua do anything. I think he would have killed her if she hadn't locked him in his room first." The words come like a flood now. I don't even know why or from where. I didn't realize I remembered all the details like the clicking until the flame took, the sound of paper burning. Fingertips singed. The smell.

God. The smell.

"She found the hole we'd made in the wall in Josh's room where we kept a diary of sorts. Everything they did to us scratched on any piece of paper we could get our hands on. We were going to expose them one day. She took them all, though, and locked him in his room, and we went downstairs to the kitchen. She turned on the burner."

Lev's eyes narrow, harden.

"She made me burn them one by one. I remember the tips of my fingers burning and the smell of it. It's weird what you remember, isn't it?"

He doesn't answer.

"You know what she used to do? They were religious, the Georges. We went to church every Sunday. She had this cross around her neck. It was a hideous thing, old and big. And when she'd watch him hurt us, she'd clutch it in both her hands, and she'd pray." I feel the rage in my voice when I tell this part. "She'd fucking pray as she watched her husband—"

I stop myself, give a shake of my head.

Lev is watching me. I see rage in his eyes too. Not pity. Thank goodness it's not pity. His grip on me is harder. I wonder if he's aware.

"When all the papers were gone, she turned off the fire, and I thought it was over, but it wasn't. She wanted to hurt Joshua. To punish him. And I think hearing my scream did it."

I don't think anything else they did to me hurt as bad as that. Physically at least. Fire is a different kind of pain than anything else.

Lev stands, and his grip is so tight now it hurts my wrists. I think he realizes it at the same moment I do because he lets go and cups my face, turning it up to his. With his thumbs, he wipes away my tears, and I think that's it when he kisses me.

I think he'll just hold me then. Make love to me. It's what I want.

But he's not finished yet because he pushes my hair back and thumbs the scar on my temple.

"This?"

"I didn't want to strip for a bath with her perv husband watching so he bashed my face into the edge of the tub. It knocked me out so I count that as a win. I didn't have to know what he did to me then."

That was the first time he touched me. It wasn't the only time there was blood, though. There was always blood with him. I think it got him off.

"I wonder if Mrs. George watched that time. If she prayed. Joshua wouldn't tell me anything. He couldn't look at me for a long time after that." I don't want to think about it, about what he was made to do.

"Katya."

I snap out of my memory. Lev's jaw is tight, eyes hard. He has murder inside them.

"He touched you? Forced you? The man who was supposed to care for you."

I don't answer. I don't have to. A single tear smears down my cheek. I lower my lashes when he won't let me look away.

"You have nothing to be ashamed of."

Yes, I do.

"Katya."

I shake my head. "You don't understand." I make myself look at him.

"What don't I understand? He touched you. He touched you when you were a child in his care."

"I used to come when he did it." I wait for his reaction. For his repulsion. I've never said this out loud. Ever. His expression, though, doesn't change.

"It's sick, huh?" I bite my lip to keep it from trembling, but I'm shaking all over now.

"That's physical. Just your body's natural reaction."

"Natural?" I almost laugh but it sounds crazed. "There's nothing natural about that."

"You didn't do anything wrong, Katya. You know that."

I look down now.

"Is she dead? The woman?"

I shake my head.

"But you killed him."

My gaze snaps up to his. No one knows that.

"You stabbed him in the gut."

"How do you know that?"

"Is that why you were sent to juvenile detention?"

I just keep staring.

"But they blamed Joshua. It doesn't make sense, though. That Joshua died the way he did because how did George do that in self-defense if he had a knife in his gut? And just the size difference between them." He pauses, and I think about Nina again. That expression she'd use of doing the math. Lev's doing the math. "What was Joshua, barely a hundred and twenty pounds was what the coroner's report said. That dick was a big guy. Did they know what he'd done to you? That the husband and wife were abusing you?"

"I don't know if they knew all along, but if they did, they covered it up because a case like this getting out would be bad for them. Kids left in a foster home where they were abused and the caseworker was oblivious, or worse? It doesn't look good. Joshua was dead, so he was the one they accused of doing the actual stabbing even though they knew it was me. I was sentenced as an accomplice, but they pinned the majority of the blame on Joshua. I wasn't fully responsible because Joshua had manipulated me, they'd said. I served my time in that detention center. My records were sealed because I was a minor, but I think also, again, to cover their asses. Those people don't care about the children they're supposed to be protecting."

"I'm going to make it slow when I kill her," he says. He traces the burned skin on the inside of my arm. "Maybe show her what this feels like."

Should I be upset by this? Tell him no? Not to do it?

I'm not, and I don't.

Instead, I kiss him. I stand on my tiptoes and kiss his lips with mine, and I realize something at that moment. And maybe it should scare me, this thing. No, it should definitely scare me.

Lev and I are bound to one another. I feel like we were from that first meeting. But it's more than that.

I think I love him.

"Stop crying, sweetheart," he tells me, hugging me to him, then sliding his hand between us to that other scar, the good one. "Tell me about this. Tell me about the day my son was born."

24

KAT

I wake up to little hands pushing the hair from my face.

"Hi, Mommy," Josh's smile is wide when I open my eyes, and he launches himself against me. I hug him tight, squeezing his little body. He smells like sleep and laundry detergent, and I can't get enough.

This feeling, I think, this is joy. And I want to hold on to it for as long as I can because I know when I let him go, the fear will creep in again.

"Pasha made pancakes!"

"He did?" I ask. Sitting up, I scratch my head as I look at the clock beside the bed. It's a little after seven in the morning, and I'm not sure when I came in here. Lev and I fell asleep on the smaller bed in what's meant to be Josh's room after making love for an eternity.

I warm at the memory. Last night, he'd made love to me. He'd kissed every inch of me, scars and all, and he'd loved me.

"With blueberries and even marshmallows inside them," Josh continues, and I guess I had drifted off in the memory of last night because I must have missed part of his sentence.

"Pancakes with marshmallows in them?" I raise my eyebrows, and Josh's huge smile makes his eyes sparkle.

He nods. "I taught him," he says, and he knows he's about to get away with it when I squeeze his cheeks, then pull him to me to hug him again.

When I touch his bare feet, I feel how cold they are. "Did you go downstairs all by yourself?"

He nods very proudly. "Don't worry, I held on," he says, trying to roll his eyes but just managing to tilt his head way back in the attempt. We don't have stairs at our house in Colorado, and I guess they still make me nervous with him.

"Isn't Lev here?" I ask, knowing he's not because if he were, he'd have put socks on Josh's feet.

"Pasha said he had to go to work. I'm going to get a toy from my room," he says and disappears.

I get up, grab a hoodie and a pair of jeans out of our meager duffel, and quickly get dressed. I brush my teeth and comb my hair with my fingers—my brush is one of the things I forgot to pack in my haste. I don't bother with makeup before making my way downstairs with Josh.

"Good morning," I say to Pasha, looking around.

"Good morning, Katerina," he says. He's a nice guy, but having him here doesn't make me feel as safe as when Lev is here.

"Where's Lev?"

"He got a call earlier. Said he'll be back as soon as he can."

"Was it Vasily who called?"

Pasha glances at Josh and gives me a short nod before returning his attention to the pancakes.

I get myself a cup of coffee and find my phone, which is on the coffee table. It's still strange not to have anyone's numbers from school or from our lives in Colorado. It's like none of that happened. Like those years didn't exist.

When I touch the screen, I see I only have 1% battery left, but before I go searching for a charger, I see the message on the screen.

Lev: I'll be back as soon as I can.

That's all. Nothing else.

I consider texting him to ask where he is, but if he's with Vasily, it's probably best not to do that.

"Do you know where I can charge this?" I ask Pasha.

Pasha points at a drawer where I find odds and ends, including several different types of chargers. I wonder who else has used this house as a safe house. Who has been here before me, and how has it ended for them?

Finding the charger that fits my phone, I plug it into the wall and turn to watch Josh eat a marshmallow pancake.

"You know, marshmallow pancakes aren't really a thing, right?" I say to Pasha with a smile.

He winks. "What do you mean? They're delicious." He plates a pancake and hands it to me.

"Thanks," I say, noticing this one is blueberry. "Did you eat?" I ask him.

He just nods, and I see how his glance gets serious when it shifts to the window before returning to the pan on the stove. As relaxed as he looks standing there, he's a soldier. He's most likely armed beneath the hoodie he's wearing, and I have no doubt he's deadly.

Just then, I remember what Lev said last night about Mrs. George. I know if we survive this, he will find her, and he will kill her.

If we survive this.

Shit.

It takes effort to eat my pancake at that thought, but when we finish, I tell Pasha I'll wash the dishes while he goes out back to smoke and make a phone call.

When that's done, I call out to Josh. "Let's get you bathed and dressed, kiddo," I tell him as a phone rings. The ringtone is foreign. I haven't changed any of the factory settings like I had on my old one, so it takes me a moment to realize it's my phone.

I go to it, see that there's no caller ID, but I decide to answer anyway. It could be Lev. I'm not sure which numbers exactly he programmed into my contact list.

But when I answer, the caller hangs up.

Under normal circumstances, I wouldn't think anything of it, but with everything that's going on, it worries me.

I put the phone down as Josh comes into the kitchen. "When will we see Emma?"

"Emma?"

He nods, and I remember that we'd made casual plans to ice skate over the weekend.

"Well, honey, they're still in Colorado so I don't think we'll be able to do that just yet."

His face falls, and he tilts his head to the side like he doesn't quite follow.

"They'd have to take a plane to get here, or we'd have to take one back."

"Oh."

"But when you see her, you'll have to tell her all about your plane ride!"

He smiles wide. "Yay!"

My phone dings. This time it's a text and I swipe the screen.

Lev: Sleep well?

Me: With you beside me, I always sleep well.

Lev: Good because I'm going to keep you up tonight.

Me: I hope so.

The sliding back door opens, and Pasha lets in a gust of cold air and the faint smell of cigarette smoke.

"I have to pick up a few things at the hardware store. That door's going to give us trouble if I don't. Can you be ready to go in a few minutes?"

"We'll stay here. I have to bathe Josh anyway."

He seems hesitant.

I put a hand on his arm. "I'm not going anywhere if that's what you're worried about."

He studies me, and I smile.

"You have my word, Pasha."

He nods reluctantly. "I'll be gone for twenty minutes. Do not let anyone in. I have the code, and I'll use the back door to enter. If anyone comes to either door, you don't let them in. You don't even go to the window. You pretend no one's home, understand?"

"Yes. We'll barely be done with the bath by the time you're back anyway."

Pasha says goodbye to Josh, and I watch him leave out of the front door. I listen to the locks click back into place as soon as he's gone and turn to Josh.

"Ready for that bath?"

"Wally doesn't want a bath today," he says.

I pat his head. "Well, that's fine for Wally, but you, mister, need one."

Josh pouts but turns to head to the stairs.

I follow but detour as we pass the kitchen. I walk quickly to that drawer where I'd found the charger because I'd found something else there too. A pocketknife.

Opening it, I test the blade. It's sharp. Sharper than most of mine and a little heavier.

And I feel just a little better about being alone here when I slide it into my pocket as I follow Josh up the stairs.

25

LEV

"Levka." Vasily gestures for me to sit down as I walk into the empty club. "Care for a drink?"

He's being unusually gracious, and I'm not sure what to make of his shift in mood. Considering the last time we spoke he could only tell me how disappointed he was, I am wary of accepting anything he has to offer. But to do so would be rude, so I simply nod.

He slides the bottle of vodka across the table, and I pluck an empty glass from the bar. Delirium isn't open yet, and the building seems to magnify every sound as I pull out a barstool and sit beside him.

"Is everything taken care of with the mess at Andrei's?" he asks.

"Of course."

"Very good."

I can't tell what he's thinking as he studies me, and I don't know why he called me here. It is out of character for him to take so long to deliver an order. Vasily has always favored using as little of his time as possible in all endeavors, so for him to call me here without an apparent reason triggers my apprehension. Regardless, I use the opportunity to ask him the question that's been burning in my mind since I left Andrei's garage.

"I know we have spoken about this often over the years," I tell him. "But this time of year always makes me think about my mother. Perhaps today, we should toast to her."

Vasily's fingers tighten around his glass, but his face remains unchanged. "Yes, I understand what you mean. I often think of her too. My dear sister, it is such a shame that her life was cut so tragically short."

He disregards my proposal for a toast, opting to empty his glass without any kind words for my mother.

"I know you told me you would never stop looking." I meet his gaze. "But have you found any new leads since the last we spoke on this subject?"

He studies me, never wavering in his expression. But in his eyes, there is an undercurrent of irritation he can't hide. And I wonder if I never chose to see it before, or if I simply contributed it to the fact that my relentless pursuit for the truth was merely an annoyance.

"I have no new leads," he says finally. "But I do believe that perhaps it is time for you to let this go, Levka."

My hand curls into a fist at my side as I shake my head in refusal. "The score must be settled. You said so yourself."

"It's an idealistic notion," he says. "But sometimes, the best thing we can do is simply move forward."

It occurs to me that he has never cared to settle the score. And now, I believe I understand why. After all these years of doing his bidding. After dedicating half of my life to being his loyal servant. Cleaning up his fucking messes and doing his dirty work. And this is what he has to say to me?

"Was there a reason you called me here this morning?" I force my voice to remain neutral.

"I'm just waiting for Andrei. Then I will explain."

He glances at the clock on the wall, and then removes his phone to check something. It's a small gesture, but it sets off something inside me. I can't explain the feeling of dread that lingers deep in my gut, but I'm starting to piece it together.

"Wait here," Vasily orders. "I need to make a phone call."

He disappears around the corner, and I pick up my phone with the intention of calling Kat. Something tells me I need to check on her. But before I even get that far, I notice a text from Pasha. He explains that he ran to the store, but he'll be back shortly. It was sent five minutes ago.

A firestorm of questions ignites my suspicions. Where the fuck is Andrei? He's never this late. It isn't like Vasily to be so patient with his time. And why the fuck did Pasha leave Kat alone? I'm not thinking clearly when I stumble out the door and into my car. But it feels like a trap. It's a feeling I can't ignore.

My fingers tremble as I jam the key into the ignition. There's no way they could know about Kat. No fucking way. But as I'm telling myself that, I notice the muddy footprint Andrei left behind. He drove my car. I never gave it a second thought, but is it possible that he found something?

No, he's too stupid for that. I keep telling myself I'm just being paranoid as I jam the car into gear and take off down the street, fumbling with my phone as I try to dial Pasha. He doesn't answer. I curse under my breath and then try Kat, but again, I get no answer.

The car accelerates, blowing through a stop sign I didn't even see. But it doesn't matter. Nothing else fucking matters. My fingers curl around the steering wheel, and I try to focus as I navigate the streets back to the house. I'm trying to dial Alexei when my phone rings, and Vasily's name flashes across the screen.

I tap the button to ignore it, and in my frustration, the phone slips from my grasp and flies onto the floor beneath the passenger seat.

Motherfucking fuck.

I kick up the speed, laser-focused on the streets. I have to get home. It's the only thing I can think of. And when I do, they are going to be all right. It won't be like last time. I won't be too late.

But even as I swallow my own assurances, I can picture my mother's face. Her dead gaze has haunted me for so many years. I wasn't there for her. I didn't save her. And now I'm failing Kat and Josh all over again. I can feel it in my soul. My heart is already slowing to a crawl, prepared to die an agonizing death at a loss I won't ever recover from.

26

KAT

Twenty minutes pass, then thirty. Josh is bathed and dressed and playing with the toys in his borrowed room.

I take my now-charged phone upstairs to check on him yet again and decide to text Pasha. I don't want to appear helpless or afraid, but there's no denying that I am anxious. He doesn't reply right away, and when that thirty minutes becomes forty-five minutes, my stomach twists into knots.

I leave Josh's door slightly ajar and go downstairs. I need to call Lev, but I don't want Josh to overhear anything.

Apart from the sounds of Josh driving the toy truck around the room, the house is quiet. I am too as I descend the stairs, phone in hand.

A sound at the back door makes my heart leap. I

hurry to the front window, staying out of sight of the sliding back door and peer through the divide in the curtains. The SUV could be Pasha's. I don't remember the make of his, just that it was a black SUV with tinted windows.

The phone in my hand vibrates with a text message and I look down to read it.

Pasha: Almost there. I'm stuck behind an accident. Everything okay?

My heart races as my brain puts things together, and this time, the sound at the back door is louder and unmistakable.

Glass cracking.

Then shattering.

I run up the stairs, the phone slipping from my hand.

"Mommy?" Josh starts, alarmed when I charge into his room and close the door, putting my finger to my mouth as I gather him up in my arms.

"We're going to play a game, Josh."

"A game?"

The house isn't very big, and a moment later, I hear heavy footfalls on the stairs.

"Lev's home!" Josh says as I try to cover his mouth.

"Shh. We have to hide now, Josh. We're going to play hide-and-seek."

"With Lev?" he asks in an attempted whisper.

I nod and carry him to the closet. It's empty but for some boxes. "You hide here, okay? Behind the boxes," I whisper, my hands shaking as I try to hide him.

"What about you?"

"I'm too big to hide here. I'll find somewhere else. Shh now."

"Come out, come out wherever you are," a man sings outside.

Josh turns his head in the direction of the sound, expression confused.

"Don't come out until Lev or I come for you, okay? Not matter what. Promise?"

"Mommy?" His eyes grow wide as the bedroom door creaks open.

I put my lips to his forehead. "Hide, baby. Hide."

I close the closet door, stand and press my back against it. My eyes on the opening door, I slide my hand into my back pocket and close it around the pocketknife.

A black boot comes into view first, big and caked with mud. My chest vibrates as I suck in a ragged breath, my stomach tight with anxiety.

The man peers inside, and I can't hide, not if I want to keep Josh safe. Not if I want him to stay in that closet because this man is looking for me or for Lev, but there's a chance he doesn't know about Josh, and I have to hold on to that.

I creep away from the closet, and when he steps into the room, it's the shiny metal of the pistol in his hand I see first. By the time I drag my eyes up to his, he's staring at me, this giant of a man, with crazy eyes and a shit-eating grin on his face.

It's the grin I recognize.

He's the one who took Nina home that night at Delirium. The man who had his hand possessively around her arm.

The one I didn't like.

And I like him less now.

Was he the one who did it? Who splattered Nina's blood all over my scarf?

"There are you," he says, looking me over and tucking his pistol at the back of his jeans as he licks his lips. "Been a while. Kat, right?"

I swallow, keeping my pocketknife hidden. I need to get out of this room. Whatever happens to me, I have to keep Josh safe.

What was his name? "Andrei, right?" I ask, playing stupid. "Lev said he was sending someone."

He looks confused for a moment, then nods.

"Thank God. I was worried," I say, trying to control the situation.

I tighten my sweaty hand around the knife, taking inventory. He's not as fat as Robert George was, but he is as tall. He's built differently, too. Like a solid wall.

And he's a trained killer.

"Yeah, uh, Lev sent me to get you." He's improvising. "Said you might be bored."

I walk toward him. "Yeah, I was." He steps out into the hallway, and I follow, closing the door behind me, hoping he doesn't notice when I turn the key in the lock grateful now for those keys I'd found strange when I'd first seen them.

"What were you doing in there?" he asks, eyes narrowing.

I'm not sure how to answer, so I distract him. "You were at the club that night," I say as if I just remembered. "You took Nina home. She said you were cute." I want to barf.

"Nina von Brandt."

His expression is flat, eyes empty. *Can I push him down the stairs?*

"She didn't think I was very cute later," he says, and I realize he's not as stupid as I hoped.

The game is over.

Andrei takes a stalking step toward me, and I run, gripping the banister and flying down the stairs so fast, I slip and tumble down the last few, the pocketknife flying out of reach.

He's right behind me, body heavy as he tackles me at the bottom of the stairs.

"You're not going anywhere!"

I can't help my scream when he grips a handful

of hair as soon as I'm back on my feet. He tugs me backward into him, the smell of sweat on him making me nauseous.

"Get away from me!" I slap at him and scratch at his face, but he's too strong and when I hear the gun cocked and feel the cold metal at my throat, I freeze.

We hear it at the same time then. The banging of small fists against the upstairs door.

Shit.

"Mommy! Mommy!"

How long has Josh been screaming?

The man shifts his gaze up the stairs, then back to me, and a wicked grin stretches across his face, making him look like the devil himself.

"Mommy?" he asks, one eyebrow cocked.

A car comes to a screeching halt outside. Does he hear it? I know I have seconds to act, and I smash my head into his nose hard.

He stumbles backward, his hold on me relaxing for just a minute, but when I try to slip away, to reach the knife just a few feet from me, he slams the butt of his gun into my temple so hard I spin and drop to my hands and knees.

"Don't you fucking dare!"

I'm dazed. My head throbs, hair hanging like a bloody curtain between us as the room spins. I think about this morning, and I can still smell the marshmallow pancakes Pasha made.

I retch then. I'm sick on the living room carpet.

"That's disgusting," Andrei says, crouching down in front of me. "Where were we?"

He shoves me onto my back, eyes like death as he scans my body, pushing thick fingers into the waistband of my jeans. He tugs me closer, forcing my legs apart and undoing my jeans, tugging them halfway down my hips.

I stretch my arm out over my head, fingers curling around the pocketknife.

"That's right. We were right here," he says, licking his already wet lips.

"This is for Nina," I say, bringing my knife arm toward his gut.

But I'm not fast enough. He hits my arm with his, and the knife clatters against the wall at the far corner.

"She wasn't so pretty after I beat the shit out of her, you know," he says, gripping my jaw to slam the back of my head into the floor. "Now it's your turn."

He flips me over, drags me up onto my knees by my hair, and he's behind me.

"Let's see what's so special about your cunt that has my cousin betraying his own blood."

27

LEV

When I finally skid into the driveway, I can't fucking breathe. My chest is caving in on me, and my vision is blurry as I head for the door. Something thumps against the floor as I punch in the code, fucking it up, forcing me to repeat the process all over again.

I have no voice. I can't even call out for her. But when I swing the door open, I realize that it isn't necessary. Because my worst fears have materialized, and I don't have to look any further to find Kat.

She's right here on the living room floor with Andrei behind her and a gun to her head. Her pants are pulled down to her thighs, and Andrei's jeans are unzipped. The first thing I think of is aiming straight for his dick.

"Andrei." My voice is a warning as I reach for the

pistol in my jeans, but before I can grab it, he's jamming his own gun into Kat's temple, shaking his head.

"Shut the door," he barks.

Slowly, I ease the door shut behind me, glancing around the room for Pasha. But he isn't here. Josh, however, is crying in his room upstairs, banging on the door. My throat narrows to a pinhole as I force myself to remain calm, meeting Kat's gaze.

She's fucking terrified. Her eyes are streaked with tears, and every time Josh cries out, she flinches in pain. It's a pain I understand because I feel it too. But I'm determined to change that, but I just don't know how yet.

Andrei is coked out of his mind, as usual, and his eyes are practically bugging out of his head. I need to get him to calm the fuck down. Keep him talking and distract him somehow.

"How did you find them?" I ask.

"You think you're so fucking smart," he sneers. "Do you think I don't know about the fucking tracker you slipped onto my car?"

I didn't think he knew about that, but I'm quickly coming to understand that Andrei isn't as dumb as he often pretends to be.

"I took a page from your book, and you didn't even think twice about it." He grabs a fistful of Kat's hair, yanking her head back to expose her throat.

She whimpers in pain, and I lunge forward on instinct, but Andrei drags her backward, bumping into the coffee table.

"Don't fucking move!" he roars. "Or I'll blow her goddamn head off right now while you watch."

"Okay." I hold up my hands in an attempt to placate him. "Just let her go, Andrei. Your beef is with me, not her."

"You were supposed to kill her!" he bites out. "You know she can't live. Vasily won't allow it. I won't allow it."

Kat's gaze moves to mine, and I can feel the betrayal in her eyes. I want to tell her he's full of shit. I want to tell her every pretty lie I can think of right now. But first, I need to worry about getting her out of here alive.

"All these years, you've been telling me what to do," Andrei continues. "Telling me what a fuckup I am. How I ruin everything. And you can't follow a simple fucking order to put a bullet in this bitch's head. You're so pathetic, I can't even look at you."

His voice is rising with every syllable, years of repressed jealousy and rage unleashing itself. I know it's only a matter of time, and he will make good on his offer. It's too late to give him false assurances about Kat. I'm caught in the web I wove, and there's only one way out now.

"Do you think I don't know how much you hate

me?" I meet his gaze. "It kills you that your father has only ever respected me. This won't change anything, Andrei. The one thing you've always wanted? It's never going to be yours. Because you won't leave here without killing both of us today. And your father will never forgive you for that."

His lip curls, and I know I've hit a nerve. But I'm not trying to provoke him. I'm trying to distract him. Because I can see Pasha at the back door now, his eyes wide as he signals to me. He's already called for backup, but I can't count on that.

"I was planning to be merciful." Andrei dips his head, breathing Kat in while she struggles to pull away. "But maybe I'll make you watch. I'm in no hurry."

"You'd like that, wouldn't you?" I choke on the words. "Your whole life, you've wanted what's mine. That's why you did it, isn't it?"

"Did what?" Andrei asks distractedly as he traces the curve of Kat's throat with his gun.

"Killed my mother."

His gaze snaps up to mine, and a sinister gleam flashes between his lips as they curl into a sickening smile.

"You know about that?"

His confirmation should come as no surprise, but the admission still feels like a knife to the heart.

"Not everything." I force the words out. "But you

may as well tell me. Because I can guarantee you this. Only one of us is leaving here alive today."

He seems to consider it, but I know he's just toying with me. If there is one thing I've come to understand about Andrei, it's that he loves to poke at this wound. For years, he's brought up my mother, a constant reminder of what I lost. But now I understand he was just laughing at his own private joke, adding salt to my wound.

I don't want the details. Not really. But it's the only thing I can think of that will keep him talking. From the corner of my eye, I can see Pasha creeping over the broken glass. He's trying to slip in unnoticed, but I don't know if he'll manage. Upstairs, Josh's frantic cries are growing louder. He's screaming for his mother, and every second feels like the span of an hour.

"Shut that goddamn kid up!" Andrei screeches. "Or I'll do it myself."

"No!" Kat screams, fighting in his grasp. I meet her eyes, silently pleading with her not to move.

"Tell me what happened that night, Andrei. Tell me what you did to my mother."

He sniffs, his leg bouncing up and down with an agitation that feels like the longest countdown of my life. I'm running out of fucking time, and he's running out of patience.

"You want to know what happened to dear old

mom?" he repeats. "I'll tell you what happened. She was a weak fucking link, just like you."

The floor creaks under Pasha's shoes during his rant, but he doesn't notice. Pasha edges closer, and I keep my attention focused on Andrei as he rages on, unleashing the story he's kept bottled up for all these years.

"I fucked her, you know," he tells me. "And she loved every second of it."

I feel like I'm going to puke, and my head is moving on autopilot. "No. You didn't."

"I did." He grins. "She threatened to expose everything she knew about Vasily. All she had to do was keep her mouth shut, but she couldn't. She'd been talking to that neighbor of yours, betraying her own family. Vasily couldn't stand the sight of her anymore. Everyone is expendable, Lev, even you."

Pasha is encroaching. I can feel his presence, but I can't rip my gaze from Andrei's. I don't want to believe what he's telling me. I don't want to accept that my mother's final hours were so horrific.

"He told me to take care of her, and he left," Andrei goes on, lost in the memory of the moment. "It was supposed to be my first kill. I had something to prove. He said there is nothing that comes before our loyalty, even our own blood. I tortured her until she vomited all over me. That was the first time I realized what I was capable of. That I was superior to my father in every way. He didn't have the stomach to do it, but I did."

"You're full of shit," I bite out.

"You're just like her," Andrei spits. "Too weak to do what's necessary. That's why we're here, Lev. That's how it all comes full circle. And now, you understand that the only person leaving here alive today is me."

My fists curl at my sides as I take another step toward him. But as I do, the floorboard behind him creaks, and his head snaps to the left, colliding with Pasha as he lunges for him. In the aftermath, everything happens in a blur.

I lunge for Kat at the same time Pasha tackles Andrei from behind. An ear-piercing scream reverberates off the walls, and it can only be Kat's. I'm trying to get to her, trying to throw my body on top of hers, but I'm too late.

A gunshot echoes off the walls, followed by another. And another.

And then, there is only silence.

***

Thank you for reading *MINE*. I hope you love Lev and Kat!

Their story concludes in *HIS*, available in all stores.

THANK YOU

Thank you for reading **MINE**. I hope you love Lev and Kat!

Their story concludes in **HIS**, the second and final book of the Ties that Bind Duet, available in all stores.

HIS

I've been in hiding for four years. On the run from the man in whose bed I once slept.

I saw something I shouldn't have seen.
Took something I shouldn't have taken.

And he's just found me.

But it's not just my safety I have to worry about. I have a little boy. *His* little boy. The secret baby of a Russian mobster.

He told me in no uncertain terms that I'm his. That we would be a family.

But his uncle still wants me dead and I know the man whose been hunting me is the only one who can keep us safe.

ALSO BY A. ZAVARELLI

Boston Underworld Series

CROW: Boston Underworld #1

REAPER: Boston Underworld #2

GHOST: Boston Underworld #3

SAINT: Boston Underworld #4

THIEF: Boston Underworld #5

CONOR: Boston Underworld #6

Sin City Salvation Series

Confess

Convict

Bleeding Hearts Series

Echo: A Bleeding Hearts Novel Volume One

Stutter: A Bleeding Hearts Novel Volume Two

Twisted Ever After Series

BEAST: Twisted Ever After #1

Standalones

Tap Left

Hate Crush

For a complete list of books and audios, visit http://www.azavarelli.com/books

ALSO BY NATASHA KNIGHT

Ties that Bind Duet

Mine

His

Collateral Damage Duet

Collateral: an Arranged Marriage Mafia Romance

Damage: an Arranged Marriage Mafia Romance

Dark Legacy Trilogy

Taken (Dark Legacy, Book 1)

Torn (Dark Legacy, Book 2)

Twisted (Dark Legacy, Book 3)

MacLeod Brothers

Devil's Bargain

Benedetti Mafia World

Salvatore: a Dark Mafia Romance

Dominic: a Dark Mafia Romance

Sergio: a Dark Mafia Romance

The Benedetti Brothers Box Set (Contains Salvatore, Dominic and Sergio)

Killian: a Dark Mafia Romance

Giovanni: a Dark Mafia Romance

The Amado Brothers

Dishonorable

Disgraced

Unhinged

Standalone Dark Romance

Descent

Deviant

Beautiful Liar

Retribution

Theirs To Take

Captive, Mine

Alpha

Given to the Savage

Taken by the Beast

Claimed by the Beast

Captive's Desire

Protective Custody

Amy's Strict Doctor

Taming Emma

Taming Megan

Taming Naia

Reclaiming Sophie

The Firefighter's Girl

Dangerous Defiance

Her Rogue Knight

Taught To Kneel

Tamed: the Roark Brothers Trilogy

ABOUT A. ZAVARELLI

A. Zavarelli is a USA Today and Amazon bestselling author of dark and contemporary romance.

When she's not putting her characters through hell, she can usually be found watching bizarre and twisted documentaries in the name of research.

She currently lives in the Northwest with her lumberjack and an entire brood of fur babies.

Want to stay up to date on Ashleigh and Natasha's releases? Sign up for our newsletters here: https://landing.mailerlite.com/webforms/landing/x3sok6

ABOUT NATASHA KNIGHT

USA Today bestselling author of contemporary romance, Natasha Knight specializes in dark, tortured heroes. Happily-Ever-Afters are guaranteed, but she likes to put her characters through hell to get them there. She's evil like that.

Want to stay up to date on Ashleigh and Natasha's releases? Sign up for our newsletters here: https://landing.mailerlite.com/webforms/landing/x3s0k6

Printed in Great Britain
by Amazon